SHERLOCK HOLMES

and the BAKER STREET IRREGULARS

CASEBOOK No. 3

IN SEARCH
of
WATSON

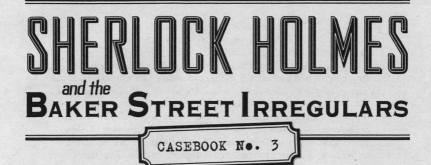

SHERLOCK HOLMES
and the BAKER STREET IRREGULARS

CASEBOOK No. 3

IN SEARCH
of
WATSON

TRACY MACK & MICHAEL CITRIN

ORCHARD BOOKS
An Imprint of
SCHOLASTIC INC.

**New York Toronto London Auckland
Sydney Mexico City New Delhi Hong Kong**

Of the many sources we consulted,
the following were particularly helpful:
The Annotated Sherlock Holmes by Sir Arthur Conan Doyle, edited by
William S. Baring-Gould; *The New Annotated Sherlock Holmes* by Sir Arthur
Conan Doyle, edited by Leslie S. Klinger; *London Characters and Crooks*
by Henry Mayhew; *What Jane Austen Ate and Charles Dickens Knew*
by Daniel Pool; *The Victorian Underworld* by Kellow Chesney;
Tower of London by Christopher Hibbert and the editors of the
Newsweek Book Division; *Bob's Your Uncle: A Dictionary of Slang
for British Mystery Fans* by Jann Turner-Lord; The *Subterranea
Britannica* society (www.subbrit.org.uk); and *The Professor
and the Madman* by Simon Winchester.

ISBN-13: 978-0-439-83671-5
ISBN-10: 0-439-83671-9

All rights reserved. Published by Orchard Books, an imprint of Scholastic Inc.
ORCHARD BOOKS and design are registered trademarks of Watts Publishing Group,
Ltd., used under license. SCHOLASTIC and associated logos are trademarks and/or
registered trademarks of Scholastic Inc.

10 9 8 7 6 5 4 3 2 1   09 10 11 12 13
Printed in the U.S.A.   40
First edition, November 2009
Book design by Steve Scott

For our parents

*"Everything comes in circles —
even Professor Moriarty. . . ."*

— Sherlock Holmes,
"The Valley of Fear"

— · PREFACE · —

Esteemed Reader,

By now, you must be familiar with the Baker
Street Irregulars, the band of loyal street urchins
who assisted the world's greatest consulting
detective, Mr. Sherlock Holmes. It has been my
mission to inform the world of the Irregulars'
existence and the importance of their work to
Mr. Holmes. If you still do not know about them,
perhaps you would care to learn from the last two
casebooks, *The Fall of the Amazing Zalindas* and
The Mystery of the Conjured Man. And there are
more tales to tell!

The year is 1890, the setting London, England. This mystery involves murder, abduction, a search for a lost treasure, and another . . . well, let me not share too much here. Suffice it to say that the Irregulars face many dangers in this case, the darkest involving deception within their own ranks. Who is a friend? Who is a traitor? Who speaks the truth? Who distorts it? And in the end, who will survive?

Since I first began my work as the spokesman, chronicler, and biographer of the Irregulars, some of you may have questioned my credentials. Am I simply another scribbler who has attributed the credit for Mr. Holmes's work to others? Who am I to tell these tales? I will tell you plainly, I was there. I knew all those involved. And someday soon, I promise, you will know my name.

For now, I hope you enjoy the story.

Yours anonymously,
London, England
1955

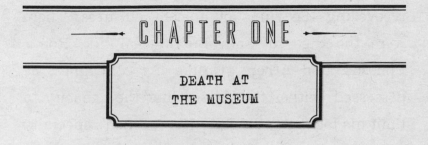

CHAPTER ONE

DEATH AT THE MUSEUM

In the semi-round reading room of the British Museum Library, Calico Finch studied the centuries-old manuscript almost angrily. He ran a silver pointer across a line and cleared his throat with a growl. He translated and mumbled under his breath before tossing the manuscript aside and reaching for another. Though gray-haired and weathered, the renowned archaeologist emanated the energy of a much younger man.

The hour was late, long past the museum's closing. But certain privileges came with Finch's station, one of which was access to the library any time of day or night.

Finch had spent the better part of his life traveling throughout Europe and the Middle East, recovering the ruins of ancient cultures. There were the digs in Wadi Biban el-Muluk, Rome, Ephesus, and Athens. Unlike his colleagues, he possessed neither the interest nor the capacity to limit his focus to a single culture. Finch's specialty was all of western antiquity!

Scanning the new page with his pointer, he sighed the sigh of a weary traveler who has at last found lodging for the night. "Of course," he said aloud, raising his head from the manuscript and pocketing the pointer. He pulled a small, thick journal from inside his topcoat. The cover was decorated with an illustration of a beautiful woman wearing a quiver of arrows and holding a bow. Finch copied down a passage.

Due to his health, he had been living in London, the city of his birth, for the past year. In the beginning, he'd been certain he would go mad. But then he remembered that every place had been followed by another and another. And then he recalled *her* —

one of the world's greatest unsolved mysteries — here in London.

Back in the forties, Finch had uncovered a Latin fragment about her, but so little substantiated it that he had soon forgotten. It wasn't until he'd found himself stuck in London that she'd nudged his brain once more. He recalled that her Roman admirers had been in this land sixteen centuries ago and had built a tribute to her — a tribute worthy of a goddess! Could the remnants still be found? Finch had grown so curious about the idea — about *her* — that, in typical fashion, curiosity blossomed into passion, followed quickly by obsession. He had studied and searched for the goddess daily, breathlessly, for an entire year. Now, at long last, he'd found the key.

So consumed, Finch did not hear the steps in the corridor until he had finished his notes. Swiftly, he closed the manuscript and buried it under a stack at his side. He shut the journal, tied it with the leather cord, slipped it back inside his coat, and stood.

He lifted a lantern from the table. It illuminated the vast library that climbed three stories high with books. He crossed the room and entered a corridor. Unsure where the steps were coming from, he proceeded calmly to the lobby, located on the other side of the Hellenic collection. There was a guard at that exit if he met with trouble.

During the last few weeks, in his wanderings through the city, he'd had the distinct sensation that he was being observed. He had been quick to dismiss the notion. After all, no one even knew about his search for the goddess. Yet, three days ago, he noticed two gentlemen waiting outside his flat in Mayfair. They were smartly attired and addressed each other as if in routine conversation. Still, they stood out against the drab street scene. One man even appeared familiar. Upon seeing Finch, the two turned and strolled away. Since then, he had been more careful about covering his tracks.

Double footsteps sounded in the corridor, approaching from behind. Finch cursed under his breath. If only he were younger, he would stand

and face them. Instead, he picked up his pace. The footsteps moved faster as well.

Finch knew they were after him. He pulled the journal from inside his coat and looked for a place to stash it. He passed the statue of a discus thrower, marble busts, vases decorated with classical figures. When he saw the open sarcophagus, he motioned to pitch the journal; it would be safe in there. But something would not let him. He kept running.

He headed for the mausoleum that he had removed from Bodrum. Four columns with Ionic caps stood atop three long stones about twenty feet high. Three statues — two men and one woman — posed between the columns.

Panting, Finch stopped at the base of the mausoleum and bent over. I *must* be the one to find her, he thought. Imagine, for centuries she has waited beneath this city and not a soul has even come close to discovering her!

As Finch stood upright, he heard a whisper from above. Looking up, he saw the bust, a gracefully sculpted torso by Pytheos. He couldn't help but admire its beauty even as it tumbled and rushed headlong toward him.

Had Finch not perished instantly from the impact, he would have spied a tall man with a high-domed forehead dressed in a black top hat and cape, staring down like a vulture.

"Carter, search him, quickly," he ordered.

"Yes, Professor."

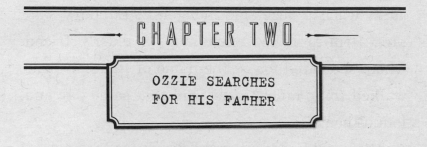

CHAPTER TWO

OZZIE SEARCHES
FOR HIS FATHER

In a thatched-roof cottage in Wroxton, England, Osgood Manning studied his great-aunt Agatha. She was resting in an overstuffed armchair by a large stone fireplace. The earthy smell of charred logs filled the room.

Ozzie prayed for the slightest tremor of understanding. But the old woman remained lost in thought, her eyes clear but distant.

"Please," Ozzie begged again. "Haven't you a clue about him?"

Great-aunt Agatha smiled vaguely, stroked the tall, frail lad's slender hand, and rocked.

Ozzie fought back tears. All his searching, his grandest hopes . . . was it all over?

He had been wandering through Oxfordshire for approximately a month, looking for his great-aunt, when a vegetable monger in Banbury said Mrs. Bentley in Wroxton had an elderly friend whom she cared for by the name of Agatha. Ozzie walked three miles in the rain that same day and found them.

His heart had leapt at the discovery that indeed it was the very Agatha, his grandfather's sister, whom he had not seen for several years. She now lived with Mrs. Bentley in a cottage outside the gate of Wroxton Abbey and looked just the same as he remembered: a well-preserved woman in her eighties with gentle blue eyes and soft powdered skin.

Mrs. Bentley had greeted Ozzie with some suspicion, but lightened when he explained his quest.

"She's my only living relative, so far as I know," Ozzie told her woefully. His mate, Wiggins, had taught him the power of sympathy, and he used it to full effect. "Agatha is my sole chance of finding my father."

Mrs. Bentley did look sympathetic, even as she shook her head. "Darling, I'm afraid the poor dear has not uttered a word for a year. Her eyes have gone vacant for nearly as long."

Ozzie's stinging disappointment so struck Mrs. Bentley that she insisted he stay for tea.

"Surely I can do something to help," she said.

That was two days ago. Now, as Ozzie sat staring at his great-aunt, willing her to speak, he still hadn't a clue about his father. All of his questions about him banged about his brain: Was he living or dead? Sharp or dull-witted? Kind or cruel? Gentle or cold? Wealthy or poor? And the old, torturous questions came, too: Why, in twelve years, had Father never once tried to find Ozzie? Didn't he care at all about his son? Trailing those questions were the ones for his mother: Why hadn't she shared more about Father? What was it she'd been waiting for his twelfth birthday to reveal? And why did she have to die before then?

Ozzie swiped at his eyes, a needless gesture, he realized, given that Agatha couldn't see his tears. And Mrs. Bentley was occupied upstairs.

Unfortunately, Mrs. Bentley had been little help to Ozzie. She knew almost nothing of Agatha's relations, other than some stories about her brother, Ozzie's grandfather.

"She was mighty proud of Winston," Mrs. Bentley had told Ozzie that first day. "Always said he had the mind to be a diplomat, but had his heart set on teaching the children." She'd rocked across from Agatha and spoken as much to her knitting needles as she did to Ozzie. "I only once met your mum, but I could see straight off she was a fine young woman, intelligent, kindhearted, and quite a beauty. Aggie always wanted to do more for her, but your mum was very independent."

"And my father?" Ozzie pressed.

Mrs. Bentley shook her head. "If Aggie knew anything about your father, she kept it to herself." She looked at her friend and sighed. "I'm afraid it's going to stay that way. Such a pity."

For the first time since his mother had died, Ozzie was at a loss for what to do. He had spent so much time and thought on his search that he had never considered what would happen when it ended. He felt hollow, as if someone had drained all the blood from his body.

He felt that way still as he held Great-aunt Agatha's soft bulky hand.

From upstairs in the cottage, Ozzie heard Mrs. Bentley call for him.

"Osgood, I found something that might interest you."

Ozzie shook himself from his daze and climbed the small wooden steps to the second floor.

From an old trunk in Great-aunt Agatha's bedroom, Mrs. Bentley had removed a large, dusty leather folder. She looked at him excitedly. "I had almost forgotten. The sweet dear would pull this out now and again."

"What is it?" asked Ozzie.

"Keepsakes, darling, keepsakes. It's Aggie's memory book. It's been at least two years since I have seen it. It utterly escaped my mind."

Mrs. Bentley handed him the folder as he knelt down beside her.

"I'll give you some time alone with it. Maybe there is something in here . . . something that will help you," she said thoughtfully.

Ozzie thanked her as she left the room.

He ran his forefinger through the dust on the cover and then opened the folder.

Inside he found old letters, pressed flowers, a ribbon, a picture of a mountain, a page from a song book, an invitation to a party from 1839, a menu, a narrow needlepoint flower, a photograph of his grandfather standing with a book in his hand, a newspaper clipping about the marriage of Queen Victoria to Prince Albert, a program to a play starring Sir Henry Irving. Ozzie stopped when he came to a tintype of his mother, wearing a summer dress and sitting on a park bench beside Grandfather. She was young and her eyes smiled at the camera, while he gazed affectionately at her. Ozzie swallowed and wiped his eyes, then removed the photo from the folder and stuffed it in his pocket. Great-aunt Agatha would never even know it was missing.

As Ozzie returned the folder to the trunk, he found some magazine and newspaper clippings tied together with a string at the bottom. He took them out, untied the string, and paged through. To his surprise, the entire stack consisted of news accounts about Sherlock Holmes. Beneath that was a copy of "Beeton's Chistmas Annual," which contained Dr. Watson's novel about the master detective, *A Study in Scarlet*. Was Great-aunt Agatha a fan of Mr. Holmes? What a peculiar coincidence!

Then another tintype fell out from between the pages: a picture of his mother, young and posed dramatically before a coach. But this time, there was something Ozzie didn't like about the picture . . . his mother appeared to be flirting with someone behind the camera.

Suddenly it struck him. All of the saved clippings were about Mr. Holmes — and his mother's picture was among them!

Ozzie raced down the stairs to Mrs. Bentley, nearly panting. "Did Great-aunt Agatha ever speak of Master?" The sharp pitch of his voice startled her.

"Who, darling?"

"Holmes, Mr. Sherlock Holmes! Did Great-aunt Agatha ever mention him?"

"Not that I recall. . . . Who is he?"

Ozzie turned to Agatha. He held up an article containing a picture of Holmes and shook it in her face. "Is that him? Is it Sherlock Holmes?!"

Great-aunt Agatha sat silently, staring off into nothingness.

Ozzie dropped the newspaper, held his head, and let out a high-pitched laugh.

"Please, darling, sit down and let me fix you a cuppa tea," Mrs. Bentley said, trying to hide her alarm.

"I must go." And before Mrs. Bentley could stop him, Ozzie was through the door and stumbling across the cobblestones, yelping like a lost wolf pup that has suddenly gained sight of his pack.

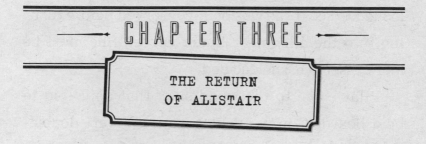

CHAPTER THREE

THE RETURN
OF ALISTAIR

Meanwhile, in London's West End, a raven-haired Spanish girl named Pilar strode purposefully down the street, wondering when she would become an official Baker Street Irregular. It had been months since their first case together, and Wiggins, the leader of the gang, had not offered so much as a hint about membership. Of course, she didn't live with the boys and didn't scrounge as they did, but she had worked on some of their more significant cases with Sherlock Holmes. And since Ozzie had left, she had been even more involved.

It was true that she'd been a bit distracted by her mother's news that they were full-blooded

Spaniards and not Gypsies as she'd grown up believing. But that was all behind her now. She looked to see if she was being observed before turning into the alley near Baker Street. She must be more assertive, she decided.

Pilar came to the wood slats that appeared to be a boarded-up window, gave the covert double-knock, and then pushed. The boards were in fact a trapdoor which opened into the "Castle," an abandoned carriage factory that was home to the Irregulars. Pilar entered a cavernous room with a dirt and cobblestone floor and a catwalk framing its upper perimeter. Two large wood doors that had long been sealed made up the far wall. A formerly grand but now dilapidated coach that they'd recently named the "Grand Dame," sat on blocks in front of them. In the center of the room a fire pit glowed. Around it, most of the boys lounged.

Wiggins, the leader of the gang, stood by the fire in the midst of a tale, his hands flying and his copper eyes shining. Pilar couldn't help but notice how easily he became all the characters in his stories.

"So Oz and me, we roped 'im good. I thought we were just goin' to tie 'im up, but Ozzie, he runs the rope into the gears and *zip*, that mad knife thrower was dragged across the ground and strung upside down like a Christmas goose in Coven' Garden!"

"We've 'eard it before," Elliot grumbled. He was a stout, surly bloke with ginger hair and scores of freckles to match. But he was sensible when it came to detective work and had a talent for sewing besides, which kept the gang clothed.

"But it's a good one, boss!" Alfie said as he brushed crumbs from his chin and jacket. He watched himself comb his silver-white hair in a shard of mirror he'd dragged in and then he stole a glance at Pilar. At seven, he was the baby of the gang and always full of schemes. Still, for his age, he was a competent investigator, and Wiggins relied on him more than on some of the bigger boys.

"Well, considering you two were saving me, I agree it's a good story." Pilar walked over to the fire pit, removed the hood of her long, velvet cape, and sat down beside Alfie.

Wiggins nodded a welcome. "The point I'm makin' is that you can do things one way or the other. Ozzie was always thinkin'. He pictured the fix in his mind before takin' action. We could've tried to tie up that crazy knife thrower, but we would 'ave had a struggle. Ozzie used his brains, his imagination, and what could 'ave been a lost battle became a victory. That's why I keep tellin' this one. We've been doin' it the hard way too much lately. Rohan, remember when you lifted that lout from the Halepi case over your head and tossed 'im?" Wiggins shook his head. "Unnecessary."

Rohan sat with his legs stretched out by the fire pit and nodded, then crossed his muscular arms. Though still a boy, he had the height and build of a full-grown bare-knuckle boxer. But his strength was a burden; he'd have much preferred smarts.

"I think it's smashin' to send a nasty bloke flyin' through the air," Elliot said, as the others laughed.

"And it did keep 'im from gettin' rough with me," James added.

Wiggins nodded with some frustration. "You boys are missin' the point. Rohan, that *was* good work. But no matter how strong Rohan is, there's always someone stronger." Wiggins pulled his hair. "If Oz was 'ere, he could explain it better."

"What he means, boys," Pilar said confidently, "is that brains are mightier than brawn. We need to stop relying on Rohan's strength and use our wits more."

"Exactly." Wiggins thanked her with a nod.

Just then, there was a creak by the trapdoor, and it opened slowly. Startled, the gang spun around to see an unfamiliar boy enter the carriage factory.

"You fellas still wearin' the same rags you was in last year? And I thought the workhouse was bad!"

The intruder had straight black hair with a single streak of white running down the front, a crooked nose, and only half a smile. In height, he was somewhere between Ozzie and Wiggins, in girth, about the same.

Who is this prowler? Pilar wondered. She noted something unsavory about him, but not outright dangerous.

Around her, the boys murmured, "It's him. He's back."

Who? Pilar was about to ask when Wiggins broke into a grin. He approached the boy and gave him a rugged embrace.

"Welcome back, Alistair! The workhouse ain't so bad. You look better than you did before." Wiggins slung an arm around his old mate's shoulder and walked him into the room. Several of the boys stood up and patted him on the back or shook his hand. Elliot didn't.

"Tell us 'ow you got out, mate," Wiggins said.

Pilar cleared her throat and raised an eyebrow at Wiggins.

"Oh, right. Alistair, this is Pilar. She's . . . she's . . . well, she's been helpin' us on a few cases."

A few cases? Pilar rattled off at least six in her mind.

Alistair studied Pilar, his brown eyes dark and challenging.

Pilar didn't like the way he looked at her. This bloke's a *mofeta*, she told herself. A skunk.

"I hope you haven't weakened the ranks by lettin' in a *twist and twirl*," Alistair said, laughing.

"Uh . . . no . . . well . . ." Wiggins stammered.

Pilar shot him a look.

"Pilar's quite smart, Alistair," Wiggins recovered. "And she's got an uncanny way of feelin' things before they happen. What do you call that, Pilar?"

"Intuition," Pilar said tartly.

Wiggins wiped his brow. "Right. Now, anyways, Alistair, we're all achin' to hear your tale."

Alistair looked about the carriage factory. "You boys haven't changed the place much. I must say, I've missed it here."

He's not very observant, Pilar noted. He hasn't noticed the tapestries I've hung.

Alistair squinted at Pilar but said nothing. Could he feel her thinking about him? Was that a warning?

"Tell us, mate, how did you get out of the workhouse?" Wiggins pressed.

Alistair turned to face the gang. " 'Twas a grand

escape, boys, the stuff of legend, I tell you!" Alistair took off his hat, revealing an *X*-shaped scar on his temple. Alfie studied it in awe. Wiggins saw jagged scars on his hands, as well.

"The house is worse than jail because they make you work until you wear away. I knew if I didn't get out soon it would be the end of me. But if they catch you escapin', well . . . it's no good." Alistair rubbed the scars on his hands.

"Finally, a few days back, I saw my chance. A skinny old man had keeled over while movin' some boulders. They put the dead in old sacks and drive 'em out in carts to be buried somewhere. When no one was lookin', I climbed into the sack with the old fella, after he'd been loaded onto the cart."

Revolting! Pilar thought.

Even the boys let out groans of disgust.

"Lyin' with a corpse?" Simpson said, shaking his head.

Alistair laughed. "It's more comfortable than you think. Anyway, when they unloaded the sack at the burial ground, they were so shocked to see me leap out, that I got the jump on 'em and that was that."

"Where did ya get the clothes?" Elliot said skeptically. "Pretty fine *these and those* for the workhouse."

Pilar nodded in silent agreement. She had more patience than most for Elliot's sour disposition. Seeing past that, she sensed a deep sadness about him and recognized that he was often capable of sharp observations. In her mind, she added to Elliot's: You look too well fed, Master Alistair, to have so recently come from the workhouse.

"Well, let's just say I was in more need than the bloke I borrowed these glad rags from."

The boys started asking questions:

"What did they 'ave you doin' in there?"

"When did you get out?"

"Where you been since you escaped?"

"What was the grub like?"

Alistair held up a hand. "There will be time for all that. You 'ave anythin' to eat? I'm starved."

Rohan tossed Alistair a roll, and Wiggins motioned to Alfie to fetch a roasted potato.

Pilar continued to observe Alistair. She thought back to what Wiggins had told her about him: that he was one of the first boys to join the Irregulars, that he was smart and could always talk his way out of a scrape, that he had ended up in the workhouse when he'd been caught stealing food from a monger. She knew Wiggins was quite fond of him, though frankly, she couldn't see why.

Alfie handed Alistair the potato. "Here you go, mate," he said proudly.

"That's the best you got? You're not still eatin' rats, are you, Wiggins?"

Alfie's face fell.

Wiggins smiled. "I've seen you cook a rat or two. But we'll go marketing for Your Highness later."

"You might say thank you to Alfie," Pilar offered flatly. "And don't chew so loudly. You sound like an animal."

"Wiggins, looks like this *fal* is trouble," Alistair said and laughed.

Before Wiggins could respond, Pilar said, "For your information, I have been working with the Irregulars for months. Mr. Holmes values my assistance as much as anyone's in this room."

"Don't mess with her, Alistair. She's harder than the workhouse." Elliot flashed Pilar a grin.

Alistair squinted at her. "A Gypsy, aren't ya?"

"No," she said, hiding her upset. "I am Spanish."

"Royalty!" Alfie added.

Just then, the double-knock sounded at the trapdoor, and Billy, Sherlock Holmes's page, stepped inside. He wore his usual blue suit with brass buttons and pillbox hat.

"Master —" he said urgently, and then stopped when he saw Alistair. "Back from the dead, are you?"

"Well, if it isn't the little tin soldier! Still sleepin' in Mrs. Hudson's hallway?" Alistair laughed.

Billy approached him, but Wiggins stepped between them. "That's enough, mates. What you 'ave for us, Billy?"

Billy sneered at Alistair before turning back to Wiggins. "Master wants you to report to the

British Museum. Someone died. Got squashed is more like it."

Wiggins looked at Pilar and Rohan. "You two come with me." Turning to Alistair, he said, "Make yourself at home, mate, you'll have plenty of company. We'll be back when we can."

Alistair stood and put on his hat. "If it's all the same, I'd like to see Master again."

Pilar and Elliot both watched for Wiggins's response.

"Are you sure you're up for it?" Wiggins asked.

"Let's move," Alistair said, heading for the trapdoor.

"What would you like me to do?" Rohan asked Wiggins.

"You best stay here."

Rohan nodded, and Wiggins was grateful for the fact that he never made trouble.

Pilar put on her cape and followed Wiggins to the door, but not before she and Elliot exchanged a troubled glance.

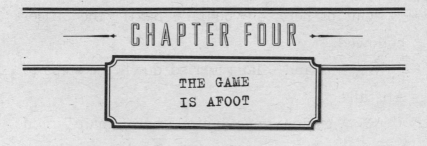

— CHAPTER FOUR —

THE GAME IS AFOOT

When Wiggins, Pilar, and Alistair reached the British Museum, the building was cordoned off by Scotland Yard officers. Undeterred, the three attempted to enter through the front doors until a uniformed arm thrust itself before them, and a voice yelled, "Halt!"

Alistair squared his shoulders. "We're 'ere to see Mr. Sherlock Holmes."

"Right, I'll lead you straight to 'im," the officer scoffed.

Alistair pushed his way through. "He's expectin' us, so you best not disregard his wishes."

At that, the officer grabbed Alistair's arm and swung him down the steps onto the cobblestones.

Wiggins scowled at the officer. "Did you 'ave to throw 'im?"

"Out of here, or you'll be next!" the officer bellowed.

Wiggins and Pilar scurried down the steps to Alistair.

"You coulda done better there, mate," said Wiggins as he helped him to his feet.

Alistair pulled away from Wiggins and spat. "I'll show that *rozzer*." He stomped to the rear of the building.

Pilar rolled her eyes. Pride mixed with poor judgment and a temper was a dangerous combination. As they followed him, Pilar whispered to Wiggins, "Has he always been so angry?"

"Last year was rough for 'im," Wiggins said sympathetically.

Pilar nodded even though she felt little sympathy. But if Wiggins held Alistair in such high regard, maybe she ought to give him a chance.

They trailed Alistair to a service entrance guarded by a police officer. As soon as the officer looked the other way, the three slipped inside, strode past a stairwell, through a large wood door, and into a corridor of the museum.

They heard voices coming from down the hall and followed them into a vast gallery where two enormous stone sculptures — each one part woman and part beast — stood some twenty feet high.

"I wouldn't want to bump into those creatures when they was alive," Wiggins said, wide-eyed.

"I think they're from Egypt." Pilar remembered seeing some pictures in a newspaper about statues that had been excavated there.

"Come on," Alistair said, agitated.

"Easy, Al." Wiggins put a hand on his shoulder. "Let me take us to Master. You're hot from that *plod*. Besides, Mr. Holmes ain't seen you in over a year. You can't just run in on 'im."

Alistair shot Wiggins a disapproving look but then shrugged. "All right, mate, it's your show." He motioned with his hand for Wiggins to lead the way.

Wiggins looked at Alistair quizzically before setting off.

Pilar decided that maybe she'd been wrong to consider giving Alistair another chance. He vexed her.

Sherlock Holmes and Dr. Watson stood before the remnants of the Mausoleum at Halicarnassus talking to a ratlike-looking man in a drab overcoat. Beside them on the floor lay a canvas tarp covering a broken sculpture and the dead body of Calico Finch.

"Has anything been disturbed, Lestrade?" Holmes said, looking about the room.

"Apart from covering the body, Mr. Holmes, I have directed that everything remain exactly as we found it. I know how particular you are about your methods."

"Lestrade, I appreciate your efforts, but allowing thirty Scotland Yard officers to track back and forth through this gallery has surely ruined any chance of discovering a footprint or other evidence concerning the murder."

Holmes pulled out his magnifying glass, approached the tarp with Dr. Watson, and pulled it back.

Unaffected by Holmes's remark, Lestrade pointed to the top of the mausoleum. "The statue sat in the space between the columns. Someone, or something, must have pushed it. It landed there." He pointed to an arm and part of a trouser leg which stuck out from beneath the broken marble. "The assistant to the principal librarian says this mausoleum and the statues have been on display here for over thirty years, so it's unlikely that the bust suddenly became unstable. And the night watchman did not see or hear anything until the crash of the statue, nor did he spy anyone leaving the premises. It's a murder, plain as day," he concluded.

Holmes lowered to his knees. "Lestrade, your observations are always brilliant in their simplicity." Holding the magnifying glass before him, he doggedly crawled about the scene, stopping and sighing and then saying, "Aha."

During this time, Wiggins, Pilar, and Alistair entered the gallery. When an officer attempted to stop them, Lestrade waved him off. Watson greeted the trio with a brief nod.

Why didn't Master acknowledge them? Pilar wondered. Well, at least he didn't pay special mind to Alistair. Her thoughts were thus occupied when her gaze landed on the broken statue and the limbs of the dead man. She covered her mouth so as not to retch. Wiggins restrained himself from doing the same. Alistair let out a whistle.

Holmes looked at him with a scowl and then resumed his examination of Calico Finch's left arm. He lifted the hand, pulled back the curled fingers, and studied them under his magnifier. He rubbed the palm with his thumb and lowered it to the ground beside what appeared to be a leather cord. He examined the cord under the magnifier and smiled, then removed an envelope from his vest and tucked it inside.

Dropping back down to all fours, Holmes rummaged for several minutes before rising again.

"Inspector, have your men clear away the debris. When they are finished, I wish to examine the body again."

Holmes then turned his attention to Wiggins, Pilar, and Alistair.

"Reporting for duty, Mr. Ho —" Alistair started, but Holmes strode past him and slipped behind the mausoleum. The three followed him to a wood ladder that stretched to the top.

Holmes began to climb. "Wiggins, please join me. The rest of you stay below." Holmes, with magnifier in hand, studied each rung as he ascended.

Silently fuming about being left behind, Pilar and Alistair watched Wiggins follow Master's heels up the ladder. The top of the mausoleum resembled a small temple with a stone floor and columns that surrounded the perimeter and supported the roof overhead. Two statues remained intact. Wiggins gazed about. Nothing else appeared out of order.

Holmes dropped to his knees once more and examined the floor before approaching the area where the bust had stood. Looking down, he said,

"It was bad luck for Finch to pass so close to this structure."

"Terrible luck," Wiggins agreed.

"Who is that boy with you?" Holmes turned abruptly and studied Wiggins with a hawklike intensity. "He looks familiar."

"It's Alistair, Master. He was with us until about a year ago and now he's back." Wiggins felt his heart pulse. He had never told Master that Alistair ended up in the workhouse. He did not want to admit that one of the crew was caught stealing.

Holmes was looking at Wiggins's face, but his thoughts seemed to have traveled elsewhere. "When did he return?"

"Today," said Wiggins.

Holmes tapped Wiggins's shoulder with his long index finger. "Your friend has come back at an exciting, or shall I say *opportune* time, my boy."

Wiggins nodded.

"That man," Holmes continued as he pointed to the resting place of Calico Finch, "had a talent for discovering lost worlds. Someone took great pains to ensure he would not discover another one. Why is that? And what world had he been searching for? The dark waters of this case run deep."

Holmes started for the ladder and motioned for Wiggins to follow. "I need you to survey the area outside the museum and report anyone who witnessed two or three men exiting the building last night."

"How do you know there was more than one man?" asked Wiggins.

"Someone pursued Finch to this structure, and someone else pushed the statue. The marks on the floor below suggest that two people might have pursued him. Come, my boy. I must reexamine the body of the ill-fated Mr. Finch and see what the librarian knows about his research. There is much work to be done."

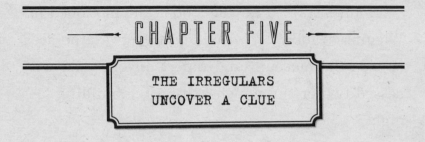

CHAPTER FIVE

THE IRREGULARS UNCOVER A CLUE

Wiggins, Pilar, and Alistair stationed them-selves across from the museum.

Nearby, an obese old man sat on a stuffed sack. He had oily gray-black hair in a matted mess and a dark face lined from the elements. Wiggins recognized him as a man of the streets. "So you know why all them police are there, mate?" he asked.

"Not me business," the old man grunted.

"How long you been sittin' here?" Wiggins pressed.

"Who are ya? Leaves me alone."

"Tell us what you know, you old *blighter*," Alistair said impatiently.

The man stood, hoisted the sack onto his shoulder with a slight groan, and walked away.

"You have a real talent for questioning," Pilar told Alistair as she ran past him. When she caught up with the old man, she said, "Sir, may I ask you something?"

The man kept walking.

Undaunted, Pilar followed. "Sir, did you see anyone leave that building last night?" She pointed back at the museum.

The old man moved quickly for someone of his age and size.

"Leaves me alone. I'm not the nights watchman."

Pilar picked up her pace. By now the boys were close at her heels. "Someone was murdered in there last night, a man is dead. Were you sitting here? Did you see anyone leave the museum?"

The old man slowed, his brow perspiring. "Those gentlemen had nothing to do with it, now push off, you little beggars." He dropped his bag and sat back down on it, straining for breath.

"Too bad, there may be a reward if you can identify the men," Pilar continued.

"You runts payin'? Give me a bob and I'll tell you what you want. Otherwise, leave me be."

"You tell us and we will bring back the man who will pay you." Pilar crossed her arms and looked the old man in the eye. "If not, we will stand here until you tell us what you know."

"*Neff off*, girlie, you have nothin'."

"C'mon. Let's leave this dirty bloke." Alistair started down the street.

Wiggins put his hand on Pilar's arm and gave her a wink. "Alistair is right. Let's go. He knows nothin'. Probably slept through the whole night and is just tryin' to get a *pot of honey*." Wiggins pretended to lead Pilar away.

"Shows what you know." The old man laughed. "I saw three of 'em leave through the museum gates together. Their carriage wasn't but five paces from me."

Pilar held back her grin. She turned to walk away with Wiggins. "I suppose you are right,

Wiggins. Even if he saw something, it sounds like he doesn't know anything."

"They were gentlemen," the old man called after her. "The one in a cape and top hat they called Doctor, no, no, they called him . . . Professor."

Wiggins and Pilar stopped in their tracks.

Professor?

Wiggins grabbed Pilar's hand and yelled ahead to Alistair as they raced to catch him. "We must find Master — now!"

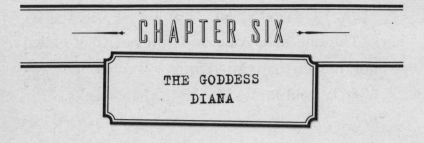

CHAPTER SIX

THE GODDESS DIANA

The three arrived at the museum breathless. They found Holmes and Watson engaged with the assistant to the Principal Librarian, Mr. Allegro Tuttle, at a table in the manuscript room. Holmes glanced at Wiggins sternly. Wiggins motioned to the others to remain quiet until Master summoned them. The clue they'd discovered was nearly burning a hole inside Pilar. Frustrated, she directed her energy to the librarian.

Thin, peaked, and bald, Tuttle was a mere rod of a man. The largest part of him seemed to be his marblelike eyes, which were magnified by a pair of thick, wire-rimmed spectacles that pinched his nose. A scholarly earnest sort, Pilar decided.

"Mr. Holmes," said Tuttle in a nasal tone, "as I have told you, the man was obsessed, secretive as well. Mr. Calico Finch did not share the subject of his research with anyone. My understanding of it is based solely upon the documents he selected and one other item."

"Pray, tell me what you have surmised, sir," Holmes said with a wave of his hand.

"Mr. Finch studied every writing and fragment in the library that contained information about the Roman presence in England from the early years of the first millennium until the fall of the Empire. He knew the writings of Dio Cassius, Eutropius, and Suetonius well, but there are lesser known fragments from those historians and other writers that are so obscure even I did not know they existed in the archive."

"But what was he searching for?" Watson said anxiously.

"I am not certain," Tuttle answered, "but I believe he was studying the Roman goddess Diana, the Huntress, the Goddess of War. There was one fragment I saw following his review that referred to Diana's popularity among Roman soldiers stationed here sixteen hundred years ago.

"Then there was the small leather journal in which Mr. Finch scribbled the notes from his research. Its cover contained a classical depiction of Diana."

Holmes removed the envelope from his pocket and showed Tuttle the leather strap he had found by Finch's body.

"Yes, Mr. Holmes, that could have been the tie to the journal."

"No journal was found near the body," said Watson. "So the killer must have taken it from Finch's hand."

Holmes did not comment on Watson's deduction. "Was there an excavation site?" he inquired as he returned the strap to the envelope.

"No, Mr. Holmes, there could not have been. Such a project would have attracted too much attention. A dig disrupts the earth more than constructing a building, and it requires many people working together. If Mr. Finch had been involved in excavating a relic, I certainly would have known. Since he often disappeared from the library for days at a time, I can only imagine that he was searching for the location of his goddess. Undoubtedly, he was still looking for her when he met his death."

Holmes conducted the interview of Tuttle for some time, while Wiggins, Pilar, and Alistair remained crouched on the floor, waiting.

Wiggins watched Alistair sigh impatiently. Though Alistair was his old friend and he'd missed him, Wiggins realized he had changed. I will have to work on him, Wiggins thought. It is like starting over with a new boy who has been on the streets alone. The workhouse has broken something.

At the end of their discussion, Holmes requested that Tuttle review all of the manuscripts that Calico Finch had studied the night of his death to see if there were any clues about his search.

When at last Holmes and Watson exited the library, Wiggins, Pilar, and Alistair followed.

Excitedly, Pilar shared what they had learned from the old man on the street. The news stopped Watson mid-stride.

"'Professor'?" Watson said, a nervous pitch in his voice. "Are you certain?"

"Yes, Watson," Holmes said unsurprised. "The very nature of this crime suggests that Professor Moriarty's hand is in it. His web covers this city. The slightest ripple of a gossamer informs him of an opportunity. It appears that Calico Finch took every possible step to keep his project a secret. Only Moriarty could have discovered it."

"What do we do now?" Pilar asked.

"Hopefully, Tuttle's studies will provide the information we seek. In the meantime, Watson and I will investigate Calico Finch's residence. Wiggins, meet me at Baker Street at eleven o'clock sharp. With Finch's notebook, Moriarty is far ahead of us in this game. We must move swiftly."

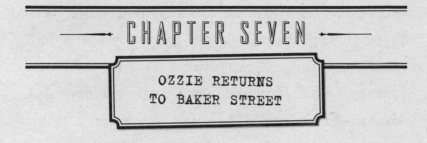

CHAPTER SEVEN

OZZIE RETURNS TO BAKER STREET

The familiar building at 221B Baker Street was no comfort to Ozzie. In fact, his insides twisted tighter at the sight of it. He fixed his gaze on the second-story windows and tried to organize the thoughts tumbling around his brain. Apart from when his mother had died, he could not remember ever feeling quite so disoriented.

And he hardly looked presentable. His trousers were covered in mud, his shirt wrinkled and stained, and one jacket sleeve was torn clear off. He had lost his bowler during his travels and his thick brown hair stood up in wild whorls. Dark circles bulged under his eyes. As he felt the tintypes of his mother in his pocket, his ears began to ring.

Ozzie had stowed away on a train from Banbury but was tossed off after a short way and walked the remaining distance to London. He had ventured through rain and cold for a day and a half before arriving at Baker Street. During the entire journey, he had obsessed over how best to approach Master. There might be little evidence, but his mother's pictures together with all the newspaper clippings, that was surely *something*. Ozzie recalled how when he and his mother moved to London, she'd always chosen jobs or flats near Baker Street. She'd also found Ozzie his apprenticeship to the scrivener on Oxford Street, just off Baker Street. Plus, didn't the Irregulars always say how much Ozzie and Master resembled each other? And weren't Ozzie's deductive powers further proof that Sherlock Holmes could be his father?

He had decided to confront Master and learn the truth. But now that he was here, he felt sick.

Gathering his courage, Ozzie crossed Baker Street. Just as he reached to knock on the door, Billy pulled it open.

"Oz! Where you been? It's great to see you, mate." Billy put his arm around Ozzie and patted him on the back.

Ozzie stepped back. He'd always been awkward with affection, all the more so now.

"Is Master in?" he asked, peering over Billy's shoulder and up the stairs.

Billy paused. He examined Ozzie's torn clothes and couldn't help but notice the strange look in his eyes. "You all right, Oz?"

Ozzie nodded absently.

"Master and Dr. Watson are at the British Museum investigatin' a death. Why don't you come in and wait?"

Ozzie shook his head.

"Have you seen any of the others?" asked Billy, cocking his head and trying to determine what was wrong with Ozzie.

Ozzie looked down at his feet and mumbled something incoherent before turning away.

Billy called his name, but Ozzie was already halfway down the street.

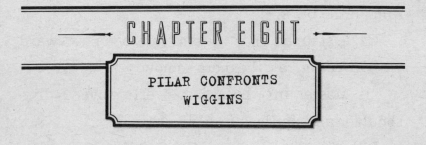

— CHAPTER EIGHT —

PILAR CONFRONTS WIGGINS

When Wiggins and Pilar returned to the Castle, the Irregulars were loafing about. Alistair had said he wanted to revisit the neighborhood and would meet up with them shortly.

Most of the boys were playing cards or eating breakfast. Pilar and Wiggins joined them at the fire pit. Elliot sat nearby sewing. Rohan was lying back in the Grand Dame attempting to decode some words in a book of Ozzie's. Alfie was stroking Wiggins's ferret, Shirley, while looking over Rohan's shoulder. "Do you think he's ever coming back, Ro?" Alfie asked.

"So you've missed me, eh?" Alistair came through the trapdoor; his voice was full of self-importance.

"They wasn't talkin' 'bout you," Elliot grumbled, barely looking up from his needle.

"Still doin' that sissy work, Stitch? What you makin', a pretty new bonnet for yourself?" Alistair laughed as he walked over to investigate Elliot's work.

Elliot pulled back his right arm to slug him, but Wiggins intervened. "Easy, boys."

"I just want to see what Stitch is makin'. No harm in that, is there?"

Elliot glared at Alistair and pulled the material closer. "None of your business."

"Watch out, Alistair. Elliot's got a temper," said Simpson.

"Alistair does, too," said Fletcher.

"A brawl is brewin'!" said James.

"All right, everyone, quiet down and listen up. A big case has come our way." Wiggins explained the events of the morning. "Go back to loafin' if you like. We need to rest up before meetin' Master."

Elliot, Rohan, and Alfie resumed their activities while Alistair rolled out a blanket near the fire pit and closed his eyes.

Meanwhile, Pilar asked Wiggins if he would take a walk with her.

"I suppose I could use some fresh air. Rohan, keep an eye on this lazy lot. And Elliot, I expect no trouble from you."

"Why you always accusin' me?" Elliot muttered without looking up. "I'm not the one you should worry about."

"You heard me, and that goes for all of you. No trouble," Wiggins repeated as he exited through the trapdoor.

Once outside, Pilar got straight to the point. "It's Alistair. There is something about him I find unsound, and I'm sure Ozzie would agree." She stopped and watched Wiggins's expression. "I'm sorry if this sounds harsh, Wiggins." Pilar paused again and then spoke carefully. "Besides that, I don't understand why you have not offered me membership. You know my detective skills rival any one of the gang's."

Wiggins looked taken aback, from her comments about Alistair or her last assertion, she could not tell.

"Well, it's true," she finished.

At least now Wiggins understood why Pilar had been after him lately. Attempting to be a level-headed leader, he just nodded as he absorbed the information. "I admit Al has changed some in the workhouse. But give 'im time. He is a smart bloke and loyal. He'll come around."

Was that a note of doubt in his voice? Pilar wondered. "Why doesn't Elliot like him?" she asked.

"Old gang history," said Wiggins. "You can ask Elliot about that yourself."

"Fine. You were awfully hard on him, you know. Is that to do with Alistair, too?"

Wiggins shrugged. He hadn't realized it was so obvious he sometimes singled out Elliot.

"Anyway," Pilar went on, "I plan to keep a close eye on Alistair."

Wiggins nodded again, but this time he kept his gaze on the pavement as the two continued walking.

"You still haven't answered my second question," Pilar said in a less challenging tone.

Suddenly Wiggins stopped. Pilar was glad he was pausing to consider her words more seriously.

But instead of answering her, he pointed to a brick wall that bordered the north side of the street. On it, someone had drawn strange symbols in chalk. Pilar and Wiggins crossed the street to get a closer look.

"What do you think it is?" asked Wiggins.

Pilar tilted her head as she examined the marking. "I am not sure, but it must mean something." She opened her cape and pulled out a writing tablet and a pencil from an interior pocket. She started to transcribe the drawings.

"You can write?" Wiggins asked, surprised.

"I've been learning in school. But you don't need to know how to write to copy symbols. With Ozzie gone, I thought I should start carrying the tablet and pencil."

Just then, the rest of the gang came around the corner.

"It must be approaching eleven," said Wiggins.

"Right," Pilar agreed, as she finished her copying.

Sherlock Holmes paced as Wiggins, Pilar, and Alistair entered his study. The rest of the Irregulars waited below. A purple bruise, outlined in red, crossed Holmes's forehead diagonally. Wiggins knew that Master rarely involved himself in rows, so something unusual must have happened.

Holmes motioned for them to sit on the settee and started in an agitated tone. "Irregulars, we are changing the focus of our investigation immediately, for my oldest friend's life depends on us — Watson has been abducted!" Holmes broke his stride, and pinched the top of his nose with his thumb and forefinger. He closed his eyes tightly.

Wiggins clamped his hand on his head and turned to Pilar, whose jaw hung slack.

"Blimey!" Alistair exclaimed.

After a moment of silence, Holmes went on. "When we left the museum, Watson and I continued to the home of Calico Finch. We searched his papers and library for clues about his work. During this time, three roughs forced their way into the residence and attacked us. As we fought them off, I received a glancing blow from fireplace tongs and lost consciousness." Holmes pointed to the welt on his forehead. "When I came to, Watson was gone."

Pilar watched Holmes with some surprise. He seemed almost emotional.

"What do you want us to do, Master?" Wiggins asked.

"We must search, Wiggins, we must search. There is a place where Moriarty's men have detained their victims in the past, the catacombs in the West Norwood Cemetery. I have arranged a cart to take you and the rest of the Irregulars there."

"Catacombs?" asked Wiggins.

"Underground tombs," said Holmes, "a quiet place to hold people captive."

"Tombs!" said Alistair. "Brilliant!"

Holmes squinted at the boy and then turned back to Wiggins. "If you find Watson, summon me immediately. I plan to investigate other avenues. We must act quickly or all will be lost."

"Do we get our normal pay or more for sniffin' out the doctor?" asked Alistair.

"Alistair!" said Wiggins and Pilar together.

Holmes paced to the fireplace and lifted his clay pipe from the mantel.

"Wiggins, your friend wastes no energy on sentiment. I hope it makes him a better investigator. Now please —" Holmes's voice nearly cracked as he waved them off. "If we save my only friend, I assure you, you will be well compensated. Now, to work!"

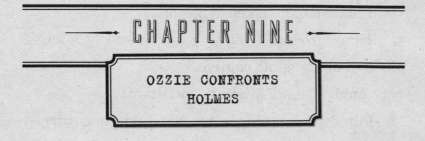

CHAPTER NINE

From his spot a few doors down from 221B Baker Street, Ozzie watched the Irregulars: Rohan, Elliot, Alfie, Pete, Fletcher, Shem, James, Barnaby, Simpson, even Shirley, they were all there. Undoubtedly, they were waiting for Wiggins, and possibly even Pilar, to come down from Holmes's flat with a new assignment. And since the whole gang had been summoned, it must be a significant one.

Ozzie felt his heart flip-flop inside his chest. Was it longing to run out and rejoin them? Or impatience for them to be on their way?

Soon after a horse cart pulled up to Holmes's flat, Wiggins, Pilar, and a boy Ozzie did not recognize exited the building. The unknown boy had a white stripe running through the front of his black hair. He looks like a skunk, Ozzie noted. The boy gestured to the others and then ran down the street as the rest climbed aboard the cart. A few minutes later, the boy returned and they all rode off together.

Ozzie looked back up at Holmes's flat. He knew it would not be the most opportune time to approach him. Master would surely be absorbed in the details of his case. And Dr. Watson would likely be with him. But Ozzie had waited twelve years for this moment! He couldn't wait a minute longer. Gathering his courage for the second time that day, he pushed open the door and made his way upstairs.

When he entered the sitting room unannounced, he found it entirely unchanged. The chemistry beakers were still arranged neatly on a table. The violin still rested in its place. Even Holmes sat in his usual chair beside the fireplace, puffing his pipe. Luckily, he appeared to be alone. His gaze was toward the flames. The only thing out of place was the bruise on Master's forehead.

Ozzie coughed, which brought the detective from his trance.

"Osgood," he said somewhat casually, "you have returned from your adventures. From the looks of you, you have been traveling for two days. What fine timing."

"Good afternoon, Mr. Holmes, I, ah —" Ozzie could feel his throat tighten and bite down on his words.

"You have just missed the others, which is unfortunate. . . ."

"I know," said Ozzie.

"They will need you. . . ." Holmes paused. "Have you seen them since your return?"

Ozzie shook his head. He fingered the tintypes in his pocket.

Holmes stood, his eyes still on Ozzie. "Pray, what did you learn during your travels in the Cotswolds?"

Ozzie removed the tintypes from his pocket and without saying anything, handed them to Holmes.

As he looked at them, a queer expression overtook his face, one Ozzie had not seen before. Was it confusion? Shock? Recognition?

Still numb, Ozzie watched Holmes carefully as he continued studying the tintypes — but he revealed nothing.

"What a lovely young woman," he said at last. "Your mother, I assume?"

Ozzie nodded.

"From the looks of these, they were taken some time ago."

Ozzie waited quietly for Holmes to go on.

"This picture of her by herself appears to have been taken in a park in Oxford. I attended University there before continuing my studies at Cambridge."

Ozzie's pulse raced. His mother, when she was young, had worked in Oxford. And Holmes had studied there! It was further evidence.

Ozzie fixed his gaze on the tall lean man before him, a man who, though complimentary at times, showed him little affection. Surely, one of the greatest minds in all of England would recognize his own son!

Holmes's hawkish gaze settled on Ozzie as he returned the pictures. He seemed to be thinking deeply.

Mr. Holmes, did you know my mother? Ozzie imagined himself saying boldly. But he could not make the words exit his mouth. If Master knew her, he would have said so, wouldn't he? Unless, of course, he was hiding something. Master was often secretive. Could he indeed be Ozzie's father but not want Ozzie to know it? And if so, why?

"Right," said Holmes, clapping his hands. "Osgood, there is much work to be done. The Irregulars are faced with what may be their greatest challenge yet. Without your assistance, I fear some of them may not survive this case."

Ozzie tried to listen, but Master's words did not penetrate or inspire him. He did not care about his work right now.

"Osgood, did you hear me? Your friends' lives may be in danger."

Ozzie rubbed his eyes. Was that concern in Master's voice? He had never heard that tone from him before.

"What do you need me to do?" Ozzie asked.

Holmes described the abduction of Watson, as well as the circumstances surrounding the death of Calico Finch.

"Meet the Irregulars at the catacombs at once. This case is different from others. The Irregulars themselves may be targets here. You boys know how to work in the shadows and observe, but how to respond when you are the game is an altogether different matter. The gang will need your quick thinking and sound judgment."

Holmes struck a match and relit his pipe. He studied Ozzie carefully, meeting his gaze and holding it. "I trust you are up to the task."

Ozzie didn't think he was but nodded anyway.

"Very good. I sense there are things you may wish to share about your adventures in Oxfordshire. When this case is over, we can discuss them. But now, you must catch a hansom. You understand?" Holmes handed him some coins.

Ozzie looked up at Holmes and wondered who he really was. Then he fled down the steps to the street, where the cold air punched his cheeks and the swirl of the loud, busy thoroughfare made him retch.

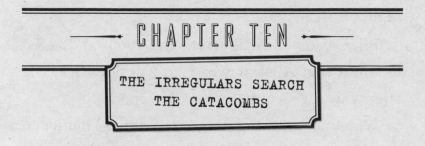

— • CHAPTER TEN • —

THE IRREGULARS SEARCH
THE CATACOMBS

The horse cart left the Irregulars in Lambeth at the gates of the cemetery. The grounds were well groomed with clipped shrubbery like in the finer parks in London. Only the rows of ornate stone crypts on either side of the paths reminded Wiggins where they really were.

Like a puppy released from its pen, Alfie ran down the path and across the lawn. His oversized ears nearly flapped.

"Doesn't he know this is a sacred place?" Alistair said.

"I doubt the people who live 'ere mind," Elliot returned.

Some of the boys laughed.

Alistair glared at Elliot. "We are workin' 'ere, and needn't be tossed out by the watchman because of that little *git*."

Pilar watched Alfie frolicking about and hated to admit that Alistair was right. Besides drawing attention, Alfie's antics were disrespectful.

Wiggins, thinking the same thing, motioned to Alfie to come back. When he did, his face was flushed from the cold. He handed Pilar a bright red maple leaf and bowed. "For your loveliness," he said, then turned to Wiggins. "I was just investigatin' the place, boss. It's safe for us to proceed."

Wiggins cuffed him lightly on the shoulder. "Elf, you just stick with us."

The gang walked the paths. Though still early in the day, a dark gray fog enveloped them and filled them with dread. They shivered in their thin outer coats and glanced about nervously, some half expecting the dead to rise from their graves and snatch them.

"You sure this is the right spot?" asked Elliot.

"You afraid, Stitch?" Alistair laughed.

At that, Elliot grabbed Alistair by the back of his coat and swung him into a shrub. He fell through it till his bottom hit the ground. His coat remained strung up on the branches.

Even though Pilar had little patience for the boys' fighting, she found it hard not to smile.

"I'll take no more lip from you!" Elliot's face burned red. He hovered over the shrub and clenched a fist above his head like a hammer.

Wiggins stepped in and pushed Elliot back. Then he offered Alistair a hand.

Alistair cursed but accepted it. Twigs and leaves hung from his clothing.

"We're tryin' to find Dr. Watson 'ere, and Master's dependin' on us. There's no time for nonsense. Elliot, if you can't work with Alistair, go back to the Castle and wait." Wiggins's voice rose with agitation.

Elliot grew redder. He stomped down the path and vanished around a crypt.

Pilar watched him go, sorry she didn't have a chance to ask him about the old gang history that Wiggins had mentioned.

Wiggins turned to Alistair. "Mate, you aren't yourself. It's not like you to mistreat people, so *bugger off*, I won't have it. If you need a break, we'll all understand."

Pilar and the others waited to see what Alistair would do.

Casually, he brushed himself off. "Aw, Wigs, I was just havin' some fun with 'im. You all seem a little softer since I been gone. It must be the girly." He smirked at Pilar.

"If you spent as much time thinking about the case as you did disrupting things, you might make a better investigator," Pilar countered.

James and Shem whistled. Even Rohan's eyes twinkled. Alfie took Pilar's hand and patted it.

Wiggins laughed good-naturedly. "I told you not to mess with her, mate." He slapped Alistair on the back.

Alistair gave Pilar a dark look, and she shot one back. What will it take, she wondered, for Wiggins to come to his senses and rid the gang of this *mofeta*?

They continued in silence down the path until they came to a chapel.

"I bet the entrance to the catacombs is in here." Without hesitation, Pilar strode through the chapel doors. Wiggins shook his head at her hastiness but motioned to the others to follow.

The chapel was small, with stained-glass windows, a few statues, some lanterns hanging on hooks, and an altar. There was no one inside.

Pilar led them through the chapel, past the altar, and into a back room where a stairway descended.

"Rohan, Alfie, and Pete, stay up 'ere and watch for anyone comin'. If we are not back shortly, go to Master and report. Do not come after us. The rest of you are with me."

Rohan and Pete nodded. Alfie scuffed his moccasins on the ground. "Boss, I want to go down and see the cat's comb."

Wiggins shook his head. "Next time, Elf."

"You blokes get all the fun."

"We need your eyes up here," Pilar assured him,

and then whispered, "you know how Pete is always losing focus."

Alfie beamed. "Right. You can count on me."

Pilar, Wiggins, and Alistair lifted the lanterns, lighted them, and then proceeded down the stairway. Shem, Fletcher, Simpson, and Barnaby followed.

They entered a wide brick passage with a long vaulted stone ceiling. On either side, every twenty feet or so, smaller brick passageways shot off. Soon they came to a huge metal contraption that climbed all the way up to the ceiling. Wiggins approached it and gazed up.

"What is it, mate?" Shem asked.

"A coffin lift. It goes up to the altar in the chapel. After the service, they lower the coffins down 'ere."

"Nice way to catch a ride," said James.

They continued on and turned down one of the side passages. Grand granite arches, each with an iron-bar door, extended down either side.

Pilar stepped up to one of the doors and held up her lantern, illuminating a brick bay. She gasped and the rest of the Irregulars crowded around her.

Floor-to-ceiling shelves filled the space. Each one contained coffins, their bottom ends exposed, two or three to a shelf.

"What kind of place is this?" said Barnaby, noticeably spooked. "Don't coffins belong in the ground?"

Pilar stepped back and held up the lantern to light the granite arch. Carved across the top was the name HENLEY. "It must be a family chamber," she said.

Wiggins, his lantern held aloft, continued down the passage. All the granite arches held bays filled with coffins.

The gang followed him, peering through the bars into each bay as they walked. A short distance down, the passage ended.

"No one is here," said Alistair. "Holmes sent us all this way for nothin'."

"We should return to the main passage and investigate each tunnel until we have searched the whole place," Pilar said with conviction.

Wiggins agreed. "It's the only way we can be certain Dr. Watson is not 'ere."

Just as Wiggins finished his words, they heard a hum coming down the tunnel.

Wiggins moved swiftly back toward the main passage and motioned to the rest to follow.

As soon as they arrived, the coffin lift began to lower. Light streamed into the passage from above, casting a fuzzy glow upon six older boys standing on the lift.

Wiggins signaled the Irregulars to scatter, but the older boys jumped off and circled them. "Runts! What yous doin' 'ere?" they yelled.

The boys were dressed in black wool suits with matching bowlers and no outer jackets. They appeared to be five or six years older than most of the Irregulars.

Before Wiggins could gather his wits, they shoved and corralled the gang into a tight group.

A giant who stood nearly seven feet tall and was presumably the leader said, "Didn't yous 'ear me? I said, 'What yous doin' 'ere?'"

Wiggins stepped forward. "Lookin' for our dearly departed," he offered as casually as he could. He had learned from his years on the streets never to show fear.

One of the older boys tried to push him back into the group, but Wiggins deflected his hands. The boy grabbed Wiggins by the collar until the giant stepped in and eased him off.

"Listen, runts, this 'ere is our land. Go back to the other side of the river where yous are safe." He removed his bowler and revealed a shiny bald head with a throbbing blue vein snaking down his left temple. He dusted off his hat and then flipped it back onto his head.

"Who are you?" Wiggins asked.

"Weez from Lambeth Marsh. They calls us the Gents. I'm the duke. We 'ave our way 'bout things, and nobody crosses us, so I'd appreciate a little less lip. Yous don't want things to get unpleasant, right?"

The duke grabbed Wiggins by the front of his coat and lifted him onto his toes.

"Let him go!" Pilar demanded.

The duke ignored her and put his face right up to Wiggins's. "What yous lookin' for?" he hissed.

In that moment, Shirley slipped out from Wiggins's coat pocket and bit the duke on the hand. He yelped and swung about. He tried to pull the ferret off with his other hand. Another one of the Gents stepped in to help, but the duke was flapping his arms about so violently that he almost knocked him over.

In the confusion, Pilar shouted, "Run!" She turned and raced toward the stairway. Wiggins and the rest of the Irregulars pushed past the Gents and followed.

As Pilar climbed the stairs, she met Alfie, Rohan, and Pete coming down. "Turn back!" she ordered them. She did not see the three Gents right behind them.

"Where do yous think yer goin'?" said one. He pushed Alfie and Pete in front of her. Even Rohan was no match for the three older blokes. Wiggins found himself wishing Elliot were still with them. Together, they might have stood a chance. But the Irregulars were forced back down into the catacombs.

By now, Shirley had released the duke's hand and run off.

Upon seeing Wiggins, the duke spit and told the Gents to shove the Irregulars along. He wrapped a handkerchief tightly around his hand.

Alistair tried to punch one of the Gents and received a fist in the stomach. He buckled over.

Two Gents picked him up and dragged him as the duke raised his good hand. "No more playin'."

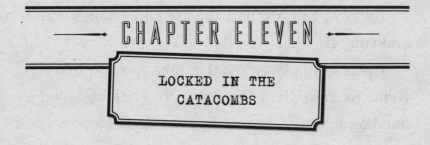

CHAPTER ELEVEN

LOCKED IN THE CATACOMBS

The Gents herded the Irregulars through the catacombs into one of the coffin bays. Alistair, still bent over, had to be pulled, and it took two Gents to muscle Rohan inside. Wiggins kept Pilar in front of him to protect her.

When they were all in the bay, the duke closed the iron-bar door, then chained and padlocked it. Gazing through the bars, he said, "Maybe sittin' in this cell will make yous want to talk 'bout why yous are 'ere. Weez might not be so polite when weez return." The duke paused and studied Pilar as if seeing her for the first time. He winked and tipped his bowler to her.

"Quit starin' at her, you lout, or I'll clobber you," Alfie said angrily before Wiggins clapped a hand over his mouth.

The duke laughed and placed his lit lantern on the ground, out of reach of the Irregulars. "When it burns out, yous 'ave to wait for us in the dark. Unless the rats get you first." He laughed again.

Stepping away from the door, the duke raised his good hand, snapped his fingers, and yelled, "Gents!" At that, the black-suited boys formed two lines and followed him out of the passageway.

"What are we gonna do now?" asked Rohan as he shook the door.

Wiggins reached through the bars and examined the padlock.

"Did you see the size of that bloke?" said James. "His hands were bigger than my feet."

"What about those clothes? They looked like a gentleman's army," said Alistair, who seemed to be recovering from the blows.

Pilar couldn't help but agree with Alistair's observation. But how could those roughs afford such respectable attire? she wondered. Either they were crooks, or someone was paying them. But who? She was considering the possibilities as she moved toward Wiggins. He had taken a wire out of his pocket and was turning it in the keyhole of the padlock.

"Can you get us out?" she asked.

"I don't know, I never really picked a lock. I just seen how it's done. I wish Oz were 'ere."

Pilar nodded. "Thank you for protecting me from those boys," she said quietly.

Wiggins stopped and looked at her. "I haven't done a very good job of protectin' anyone, or we wouldn't be in 'ere."

He went back to his work.

The lantern cast a dim light in the chamber. As Wiggins worked and the other boys huddled together grumbling, Pilar looked around. Coffins lined the shelves on one wall. There did not appear to be a way out.

"Wiggins," she said, "I think we should see if there are any vents we can use to escape."

Wiggins pocketed the wire in frustration. "Good idea."

Pilar put a hand on Alfie's shoulder. "We need you to climb the shelves and see what's in there."

"Between the coffins?" Alfie squeaked.

"You're the only one who can fit," said Pilar, and then added in a whisper, "and you are braver than the rest of this lot."

Alfie grinned proudly. "Right. Where do we start?"

The first shelf was only a few feet off the ground. Alfie scurried up and slid between two coffins. After a few minutes, he crawled back out, shaking his head.

"Nothin' in there. The walls are solid."

Rohan hoisted Alfie up to the next shelf and the one after that. Each time, he came back shaking his head.

As Wiggins waited for Alfie's next return, he wondered how the Gents knew they were here. Had they been followed? He hadn't seen anyone on the streets watching them before they entered the cemetery or anyone in the cemetery either. If they hadn't been followed, how did the Gents know where to find them? And where was Elliot?

The lantern grew dimmer. How long would it be before they were swallowed by complete darkness?

"Maybe we should yell for help," said Fletcher.

"No one would 'ear us all the way down 'ere," said Simpson.

"And it might just bring those Gents back sooner," said Alistair.

Alfie climbed off the last shelf and shook off the dust and cobwebs.

"What are they goin' to do to us when they come back?" asked Pete.

"What if they *don't* come back . . . ?" said Barnaby. "We'll starve."

"Don't worry, mate. When this is all over, I'll cook up a feast to celebrate our escape from those Gents," Wiggins promised. But his voice didn't sound convincing, even to himself.

Just then, a lantern light came bobbing down the corridor toward them.

Wiggins motioned to the Irregulars to be silent.

Slowly, the glow grew closer. When at last it approached, several Irregulars gasped, as if seeing a ghost.

"Ozzie!" yelled Alfie.

The rest of the gang crowded around the door and talked over one another.

"What are you doin' 'ere?"

"How did you find us?"

"You look awful."

"You're even skinnier than before."

"What happened to you?"

Wiggins quieted them and stuck his hand through the bars. Ozzie shook it. "Welcome back, mate!"

"Now that's a more proper greeting." Ozzie held up the lantern and grinned. Shirley was perched on his shoulder.

"How did you know where to find us?" Wiggins asked.

"Master —" Pilar and Ozzie said at the same time, and laughed.

Pilar studied her friend. His eyes looked sunken, his cheeks hollow, and something about him seemed distant. Still, she felt herself relax in his presence. Surely Ozzie would be able to get them out of here.

"After Master paid my transport here," Ozzie said, "Shirley led me to you. She knows the smell of *bangers* on Wiggins's fingers like she knows her own name."

At that, Shirely climbed off of Ozzie and scurried over to Wiggins who scooped her up and cradled her.

"How did you end up in here?" Ozzie asked, examining the door lock.

Wiggins explained the events of the past hour.

Meanwhile, Alistair pushed his way to the front. "Who's this?"

"This is the famous detective, Osgood Manning." Wiggins made a grand sweep of his arm. "He has just returned from an important search, which we'll talk about after he helps us get out of 'ere. Any ideas, Oz?"

"Hang on." Ozzie disappeared down the passage and returned a minute later dragging a sledgehammer. "This should do the job."

"If you can lift it." Alistair laughed.

Ozzie put down his lantern and heaved the hammer onto his shoulder. His knees buckled from the weight of it.

When he regained steadiness, he swung the hammer down. It hit the chain but missed the lock. Both Ozzie and the hammer slammed the ground with a solid thud.

Alistair laughed again. "This bloke's definitely not famous for his strength."

Alfie and Pilar glared at him. But Ozzie just stood and tried again. This time he missed the lock and chain entirely and hit the wall, which set off a spark.

"Keep trying," Pilar encouraged.

By now, Ozzie was panting from the effort. For the first time since he'd been back, he realized how tired he was from his travels. His body ached to lie down and sleep.

"We'll never get out of here," said Alistair bitterly.

"Not with that attitude," Pilar growled.

"Come on, Oz," Wiggins encouraged him. "Let's all go home and I'll roast us some bangers."

Ozzie grinned and lifted the hammer one more time. "Ayyy!" he groaned as he brought it down. The hammer hit the lock right at its joint. It split open. Ozzie slammed the dirt from the momentum.

The Irregulars howled with excitement as Rohan and Wiggins pushed open the iron door and helped Ozzie to his feet. "Nice work, mate!"

Pilar hugged him. He was too tired to be embarrassed.

"Come on. We have to search for Dr. Watson," said Wiggins.

"There are more lanterns at the end of this passage," Ozzie told him. "If we split up, I am sure we can search the place swiftly."

"What about the Gents?" said Alfie.

"Let's be quick about it," said Wiggins as he waved the others to follow.

The catacombs were less mazelike than the Irregulars thought. The main passage had four smaller passages that shot off on either side. Each of the smaller passages contained ten chambers.

The group split up. In the center of the main passage, Ozzie, Wiggins, and Pilar came upon a stone arch that rose ten feet from the floor. It was made of brick and stone but was more worn than anything else down there.

"What do you make of it?" said Wiggins.

"It looks quite old, ancient actually," Ozzie observed.

They were circling the arch and studying it when the rest of the gang arrived. No one had located Watson.

Following Wiggins's instructions, they returned to the stairway and moved quietly, listening for the Gents as they made their way up to the chapel.

Once inside, Ozzie's eye was drawn to a statue with a velvet cloth resting beneath it. The cloth had been folded oddly — in the shape of an arrow. Ozzie flipped up the corner and discovered several folded sheets of paper. Carefully, he opened them. His brow furrowed as he studied the words inside.

"What is it, Oz?" Wiggins asked.

"I recognize this handwriting," said Ozzie. "It's a message from Dr. Watson."

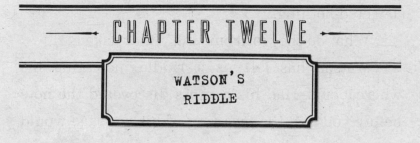
Where: William's square, circled twice, nineteen in one, the princes. What: all's Well that ends Well. Why: next."

Holmes read the sheet of paper for a second time as Ozzie, Pilar, and Wiggins sat before the fire warming their hands. Wiggins had sent the rest of the gang — including a protesting Alistair — back to the Castle. Holmes placed the paper, along with the blank sheet that accompanied it, on the mantel and paced the room.

"Ah, Watson, you are still well," he said with a relieved sigh. "And you left us a clue to where they are taking you."

Ozzie watched Holmes carefully to see if he acted any differently toward him, but he detected nothing.

"What do the words mean?" Pilar asked.

"Watson has left us a riddle indicating his whereabouts. Had his captors discovered the note before you did, the meaning of his message would not be clear to them."

Holmes turned to Ozzie. "What do you make of it, Osgood?"

Snapping to attention, Ozzie stood and took the pages from the mantle. A nervousness rose in his chest. Perhaps if he impressed Master, he would be more willing to speak openly about the past.

"The writing is most definitely Dr. Watson's, though it is messier than usual. I don't understand why because it does not look as though it was written hastily, nor do the letters suggest any agitation on the Doctor's part. The scrawl looks intentional."

Holmes watched Ozzie but remained expressionless. "Those months as a scrivener's apprentice and forger gave you a valuable tool, Osgood. Pray, continue."

"The riddle is more of a puzzle for me. 'William's square, William's square' . . ." Ozzie stared at the bullet holes in the wall, concentrating.

Wiggins watched his friend, amazed by his powers. As they'd returned from the cemetery, Ozzie had explained about not finding his father, but he seemed distracted, like he was holding something back. Wiggins was happy to see that now, in front of Master, he was more himself.

Pilar broke the silence. "Could it be William the Conqueror?"

Ozzie turned to her, as did Holmes and Wiggins.

"I read about him in school," Pilar explained. "Surely Dr. Watson refers to a famous William. And William the Conqueror was very famous. He won the Battle of Normandy and brought the French here to England."

Holmes gave a slight nod, one of approval, Pilar thought.

Wiggins nodded. "But what's his 'square'?"

Ozzie's eyes sparked. "The original part of the Tower of London is square, and it was built by William the Conqueror!"

"Excellent, Irregulars," said Holmes.

Pilar smiled. It was the first time anyone had referred to her as an Irregular — and Master himself had said it! Pilar's satisfaction was not lost on Wiggins, who would not meet her gaze.

Holmes continued. "The Tower of London consists of many towers and walls. The original castle — the white square structure at its center — was erected by William the Conqueror some eight hundred years ago. Two walls circle it. Nineteen towers rise up from the site. Watson's riddle is, in fact, quite simple: 'William's square, circled twice, nineteen in one' — of course it is the Tower.

"Now," said Holmes, "can you decipher the rest of it?"

Ozzie, Pilar, and Wiggins sat silently. Why was Master testing them like this? Wiggins wondered. Why would he delay the search for his friend? He crossed his arms impatiently.

Holmes paused a minute more. When there was no response, he said, "One of the more famous Towers is called 'The Bloody Tower.' Years ago, two young princes were held there in captivity. Watson is citing the area within the complex where he believes he will be held."

Ozzie read the message again, "'All's Well that ends Well.' Perhaps we should be looking for a well of some sort."

"Exactly," Holmes said. "The capitalized words in that phrase are a directive. The last clue, 'next,' tells us that the next place they will take Watson is the Tower. And that is where your search will continue."

"Why would they take Dr. Watson there?" Pilar asked.

Holmes paced to the windows. "You are not to approach Watson's abductors under any circumstances. Observe and report, that is all. If you come across your acquaintances, the Gents, leave the area immediately," Holmes warned.

Pilar crossed her arms. Why had Master ignored her? And why was he lounging about his flat when his friend had been kidnapped? This case was growing more and more peculiar.

Ozzie was having similar thoughts as he read the newspaper headline on Master's coffee table: "Assistant to Sherlock Holmes Missing! Scotland Yard Investigates."

Inspector Lestrade had departed from Holmes's flat when they'd arrived. Why were he and the Irregulars engaged in the search but not Master?

Holmes turned to face them, his gaze piercing. "We will not help Watson's situation if you are taken, too. Do you understand?"

They all nodded and then stood to leave.

Holmes lifted his pipe. "Irregulars, this case demands cooperation and loyalty. Watch out for one another and stay together."

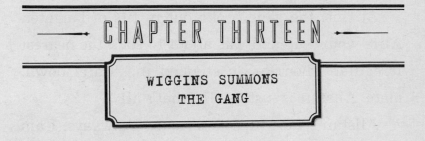

CHAPTER THIRTEEN

WIGGINS SUMMONS THE GANG

Alistair stood on top of the Grand Dame, staring down at the rest of the boys. "Where is that fat bloke?"

"It is strange he ain't here," agreed Barnaby.

"Elliot's just mad. He'll be back," Rohan assured them.

Alfie, for his part, had just finished scrubbing his hands and face in a bucket of cold water and was busy trying to wet down an unruly cowlick. He studied it in frustration in the mirror.

"Look at little Elf, tryin' to impress that bird, Patty," Alistair chided.

"Her name is Pilar," Alfie shot back. "And don't you be callin' her a bird. She's a princess."

At this, the gang broke out in fits of laughter. Alfie wound up and was about to sock the nearest Irregular when Rohan stepped in. "Calm down, mate. Alistair is just teasin', that's all."

Alistair's face turned serious. "Anyways, I am tellin' you, Elliot runs off and the next thing that happens is those Gents appear. What's that tell you?"

"That he 'as good timin'," said Wiggins as he, Ozzie, and Pilar entered the Castle. "Alistair, don't start trouble. Elliot's been in the gang as long as any of you, and he's trustworthy. He has an ill temper, that's all."

"Yeah, but from what I remember, Stitch lived in Lambeth Marsh, just like those Gents," Alistair shot back.

"That's true," said James, and a few of the other boys nodded.

"Enough," said Wiggins. "We all come from someplace. We can't be doubtin' each other now.

Anyways, Elliot ain't 'ere. So let's get to work. Master wants us to search for Dr. Watson at the Tower of London."

"I'll wait for you outside," said Alistair angrily as he hopped down from the carriage and stormed out the trapdoor.

Wiggins shook his head. "Okay, boys, grab a few lanterns. We may be headin' back underground."

"I'm ready for our next adventure, boss," said Alfie, eyeing Pilar and wondering if she noticed how clean he looked.

Pilar smiled at him. Then she turned to Ozzie. "Are you up to it?"

But Ozzie's thoughts were still with Master. When they had exited his flat, Ozzie looked up and saw the detective staring down at them. Was he watching *me*? Or was he just concentrating and not seeing any of us?

Wiggins gave Ozzie a light shove. "We need you here with us, Oz. I know you're tired from your trip, but we got to find the Doctor."

Ozzie coughed and followed Wiggins back toward the trapdoor.

Pilar and Wiggins exchanged a concerned look before they all headed out into the stinging afternoon air, where dark clouds hovered like a warning.

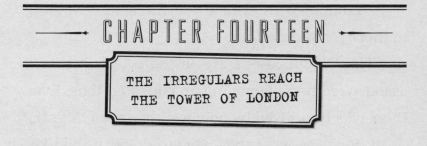

CHAPTER FOURTEEN

THE IRREGULARS REACH THE TOWER OF LONDON

The Tower of London loomed high above the River Thames. Yeoman Warders, dressed in red-trimmed blue uniforms and matching hats guarded the entrance to the Middle Tower. A few of them held long shafts with axelike blades at the top. Even though the fortress was guarded, people seemed to casually come and go through the gate.

"They call them Beefeaters," said Ozzie as the gang approached. "Possibly because they receive large rations of meat."

"Now there's a job for you, boss," said Alfie, grinning.

A few of the others laughed.

Even Wiggins couldn't help but chuckle as he

motioned to the gang to follow him toward the gate.

A Yeoman Warder held out his arm. "Nothing in there for you urchins."

"The Crown Jewels are in there, aren't they?" asked Wiggins, summoning an educated tone. Even Pilar was impressed by how well he carried it off.

"I don't see what they have to do with the likes of you," the guard sneered.

"Well, I'm a subject of this realm," said Wiggins with a slight bow, "which gives me, Mr. Beefeater, the right to see Her Majesty's baubles."

Another Yeoman Warder smirked, but the one Wiggins had addressed raised his shaft. "Out of 'ere, you little rats — all of you!"

The Irregulars backed away from the gate.

"Look," said Alfie, "children just like us are walkin' in there."

"They are rich and have parents, so they ain't just like us, you *wally*," said Alistair.

Wiggins looked up at the imposing stone walls that circled the Tower complex and then at Ozzie. "You have any ideas, mate?"

"Dr. Watson couldn't have been led against his will past those Beefeaters. There must be another entrance. Let's circle the walls."

As they did so, they discovered an empty moat that surrounded the Tower. The water had been drained and replaced with a wide strip of bright green grass. Following Ozzie's lead, the Irregulars made their way down and circled the Tower, gazing up at the battlements as they went.

They passed two large wood gates, their hinges bolted into the walls of the fortress. An iron latch locked the gates at the center. A Yeoman Warder stood on the other side.

"Wait," Wiggins whispered. " 'Ave a look there."

Above the gate, workmen were renovating a residence. The gang could see carts, ladders, tools, stacked timbers, and a horse cart with a long bed for hauling them. The driver of the cart was backing it around until the horses faced the gate. The Yeoman began to unlatch it.

Wiggins gathered the Irregulars together. "Mates, we need the dodge and sprint. You remember how it's done? Pilar and Oz with me, the rest of

97

you sprint. Now pass over the lanterns. We'll need 'em."

"What about me?" asked Alistair.

Wiggins shook his head. "Just us three. Any more is too many. Anyways, Al, I remember you as a fast runner."

Alistair turned and spit.

"I want to go with you, too," Alfie complained.

Wiggins held up a hand to silence him as the Yeoman Warder opened the huge latch. A few workmen helped him open the gates so the horse cart could pass through.

"Now!" said Wiggins.

The sprinters howled and raced toward the gates, then made a sharp right turn into the Tower complex. The Yeoman and a few workmen gave chase.

Meanwhile, Wiggins whistled a jaunty tune as he, Ozzie, and Pilar swung their lanterns, strode past the horse cart, turned left, and casually entered the complex.

CHAPTER FIFTEEN

SEARCHING THE TOWER

Where should we start?" asked Ozzie.

"We have to find the Bloody Tower and the well," Pilar reminded him as she and Wiggins exchanged another worried glance.

Pilar sympathized about Ozzie's father. She knew from experience how terrible it felt not to know your history or where you came from. She gave his arm a gentle squeeze as she led them between two vast walls with turrets and towers rising on either side. They proceeded through a stone archway and entered another section of the fortress within the second wall. Here, there were newer Tudor buildings as well as others like the ancient main fortress.

When they came upon a series of decaying arches, Ozzie crouched down to rest. His breathing was labored. He pulled out his tonic and took a swig. "Do you know anything else about this place?" he asked Pilar.

"Not much. Except that the Tower of London was built on the ruins of an old Roman fortress." She touched one of the arches.

The word "ruins" clung to Ozzie's brain.

"The brick and stone is the same as that arch in the catacombs," Wiggins noted. "What's goin' on 'ere?"

That's it. *Roman* ruins, again, Ozzie thought. Calico Finch, he thought.

They kept on and passed a few well-dressed people admiring various details in the architecture. Ozzie, Wiggins, and Pilar paused to consider some of them, and that's when they saw him, not twenty feet away. His height, black suit, and bowler were unmistakable.

"Blast it!" Wiggins growled. "How do those Gents know our every move?"

"It looks like the duke brought along two cohorts," Pilar whispered. "I don't think they've spotted us."

The three ducked their heads, and she guided them quickly through the ruins until they came to a cistern.

Wiggins peered down into the hole in the ground.

"The well," said Ozzie.

"How do you know that's what it is?" Wiggins asked.

Pilar pointed to a sign that read WELL.

"If Dr. Watson is here, this is where we'll find 'im, right?" Wiggins looked around to see if anyone was watching. Then he stepped down into the crater. Ozzie and Pilar followed. They crept across a large stone ledge and two smaller ledges. Then they lit the lanterns and stepped into the darkness.

The cavern had been carved out of stone and clay. Ancient columns were imbedded in the walls.

"More ruins," said Pilar.

They moved through the cavern until they heard voices.

Wiggins motioned to Ozzie and Pilar to turn down the lanterns. Silently, they edged their way to a large, dimly lit chamber where two men stood conversing, their frames cast in silhouette.

The dank air pressed on Ozzie's lungs. He covered his mouth but could not keep a cough from escaping.

The figures turned and raised their lanterns.

"Who is there?" one asked, a quaver in his voice.

Wiggins thought he recognized the voice from somewhere.

"Show yourselves!" said the other figure in a commanding tone.

When no one did, the two men turned and ran up a stairway.

"What now?" asked Pilar.

"Follow them!" said Wiggins.

Ozzie stood motionless.

"Oz," Wiggins said in frustration. "Let's go! They are gettin' away."

But Ozzie did not take a step.

Pilar put a hand on his shoulder. "What is it?"

"The second man who spoke," said Ozzie. "That was Dr. Watson."

CHAPTER SIXTEEN

CIPHERS ARE
DISCOVERED

Swiftly, they exited the Tower complex through the middle gate. None of the Irregulars were in sight, nor were the Gents or Watson.

Pilar pressed on her left eye to stop it from twitching. "What is this all about? If that was Dr. Watson, why did he run? And he sounded perfectly well. He wasn't a prisoner."

Wiggins nodded. "He was talkin' to that gentleman like he was a mate. And the other voice — I 'eard it before."

"Me, too," said Pilar.

Ozzie's mind raced. He had ideas, but he didn't like the conclusions he was drawing. "None of it makes sense," he said wearily. "Maybe I was wrong, maybe that wasn't Watson."

"It ain't like you to be wrong about somethin' like that, Oz," said Wiggins.

"This whole search puzzles me," Pilar admitted.

Ozzie rubbed his eyes. "Master is acting out of character. I don't think he's sharing all the facts with us."

"He doesn't always share the facts," said Wiggins.

"But if he's lying to us, we should confront him," said Pilar.

"Really?" said Wiggins, his patience thinning. "I don't think Master would like that."

Ozzie recalled his poor attempt to confront him earlier and felt his stomach roil.

"If Sherlock Holmes ain't tellin' us the whole story, he's got a reason — and that's good enough for me."

"Yes, but why is he making things up?" Pilar pressed. "If we *knew* the reason perhaps we could do more."

She and Wiggins faced off in cold silence.

Meanwhile, Ozzie's thoughts tumbled back and forth from the conversation he still wanted to have with Master to the case.

"The voice," said Pilar suddenly. "I know the voice of the other man, it was —"

"— the assistant to the Principal Librarian from the British Museum!" Wiggins finished. "Mr. Tuttle."

Ozzie nodded as the pieces put themselves together in his mind. "This is all about Calico Finch's death," he thought aloud. "Holmes invented Watson's abduction, as a distraction."

"For whom?" Pilar asked.

Ozzie stood, feeling more energized than he had all day. "There's only one way to find out."

Holmes was not in his flat when they arrived. Frustrated, Ozzie told Billy to summon them right away when he returned. He, Wiggins, and Pilar headed back to the Castle, each harboring private thoughts. Then, just as they turned off of Baker

Street and walked a short way, Wiggins noticed chalk marks on the wall of a building. "There they are again." He pointed them out to Ozzie.

⊙⊠⊡⬚.⊟▱⊙⊛▱⊟⊖○◫⊗.▱⊖.△⬚⊗⊙.
◑⊖⊘△⊖⊕⊞.⊟▱○⬚⊙⊛▱⊘△.

Pilar pulled out her writing tablet and scribbled them down. Then she compared them to the last series of symbols she'd copied. "Some are the same, but there are new ones, and they are in a different order."

Ozzie's gaze traveled from the tablet to the wall. "These are definitely messages. They're ciphers."

"What's a cipher?" Wiggins asked.

"The symbols stand for letters and make up words. If we can figure out which symbol is which letter, we might be able to see what it means."

"There's another," Ozzie said, crossing the street.

⊙⊠⬚.⊙⊖△⬚⊘.⊖◿.⊠⊖○⊞⊖◑.
⊙○⬚◿⊘.⊕⊟⬚⊟⬚.⬚⊗.⊞⊖△◑.

⊕□◪.⊗⊛⊘◪◪◭.□◐⊞.⊛□◊◔⊙⊠◪.
⊛□◪.□⊠⊠◪△.

"But what does all of this have to do with us?"
Wiggins said wearily. He needed a meal.

"Maybe nothing," said Ozzie, gazing at another
building farther down the street. "There's more."

Pilar and Wiggins followed.

They saw:

⊘□◪⊙⊛□◐.◪oo◪⊞⊞◪□⊛◪⊠◭.

"This one looks like it was written by someone
else," Ozzie observed.

Wiggins examined it. "How can you tell?"

"The chalk is a different color and the handwriting is rougher."

Pilar finished her copying and looked at the
boys. "We are quite close to the Castle now, so it
must have to do with us."

The thought weighed on all of them as they
walked home. A frigid afternoon wind reddened
their ears and cheeks.

Moments later, Alfie darted out of the alley, yelling, "Wiggins, come quick!"

As he drew closer, Wiggins could see that his eyes were wet with tears. "What is it, mate?"

"It's been wrecked — all of it, even the Dame."

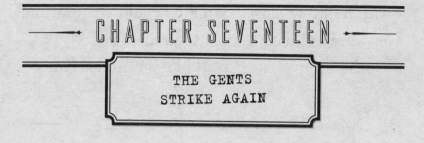

Splintered pieces of wood littered the floor of the alley. The planks to the trapdoor were ripped apart. Inside the carriage factory, clothes, blankets, cooking sticks, stools, and crates lay smoldering in the fire pit. Plates and glasses were shattered on the floor. Tomatoes splattered the walls. The Irregulars' precious books and magazines were now little more than shreds.

Worst of all, the grand carriage that had been used as a stage, sleeping compartment, lounger, and source of more than a few imaginary adventures had been knocked off its blocks onto its side. The doors had been torn clear off, the stuffing from the seat cushions projected in elongated puffs through the torn fabric. In tar, spread across the far wall with an old broom, was written GENTS.

Wiggins gazed about the only home he had ever known — now in ruins. All of their possessions were broken or missing. What little comfort he had managed to create was gone.

Rohan walked calmly through the debris, picking up pieces of things to see if there was anything worth saving and then throwing most of them into the fire pit.

"Bloody Gents," Alistair said. "They'll pay."

Pilar stood numb, at a loss for what to do. Alfie walked over to her, and she offered him her hand, which he laid his cheek upon.

Wiggins felt a knot clog his throat and choked back tears. Then, like a wounded animal, he let out a mournful howl.

Ozzie watched the scene in a slight daze, his mind clicking, trying to piece together the events of the day. He was certain now that they were all related — the ciphers, the Gents, Calico Finch — he just did not know how.

You've survived worse than this, Wiggins told himself, remembering all those shivering nights passed in dark alleys with no cloak and no company. He swiped at his tears. "Okay, mates." His voice cracked and he swallowed and tried again. "It's a bloody mess, and we'll be better off if we just clean out the place and start over. Barnaby, you're a good hand with the tools, you and Pete go find some nails and a hammer and work on the trapdoor. The last thing we need is others comin' in 'ere. Rohan, build up the fire and burn what you can. The rest of you, find a way to make yourselves useful."

"What about the Grand Dame?" asked Alfie.

Wiggins looked at the damaged coach and shook his head. "Leave her be for now. When this case is over, we'll fix her if we can."

Absently, Ozzie helped clean, his mind still reeling. After a while, he asked Pilar for the writing tablet and a pencil and climbed up to the catwalk. He studied the ciphers and tried to remember the rules. Master would know exactly where to begin. He was a skilled cryptologist who had broken countless codes. Ozzie remembered watching him decipher a few. Examining the symbols now, he knew they were the key to everything.

CHAPTER EIGHTEEN

A SPY IS SUSPECTED

There is a spy among us," Ozzie told Wiggins.

The two were out for some air after a few hours of cleaning.

"What are you talkin' about, Oz?"

"Just what I said. One of the Irregulars is a spy."

At first, Ozzie had been baffled by the ciphers, but then he found the right vowel-symbol combination and the code seemed to unlock itself. When he read the messages in their entirety, his heart raced. He knew he had to keep his composure in front of the others and approached Wiggins casually.

"Blast it!" said Wiggins. "I don't want to hear it, mate. Today has been too much. The Castle's destroyed, Master is lyin' to us about Dr. Watson's abduction, Alistair is causin' more trouble than I need, I don't even know where Elliot is, Pilar is pesterin' me to join the gang and the others ain't gonna like that. And to be honest, you been actin' mighty strange yourself since you returned. And now you're tellin' me that one of us is a spy!"

Wiggins grabbed his hair, spun around, and dropped down to the walkway.

Ozzie sat down next to him and awkwardly patted his shoulder.

Wiggins rubbed his eyes. "You really think there's a spy?"

"Those chalk symbols are messages. Three of them were written to the Gents, letting them know about our investigation, where we were going today, and the location of the carriage factory. Look." Ozzie showed him the notebook:

[cipher symbols]

Holmes knows he did it and about the journal.

[cipher symbols]

The catacombs at West Norwood Cemetery.

[cipher symbols]

The Tower of London. Their place is down the street and through the alley.

Ozzie continued, "The fourth one was written by a Gent to the spy."

[cipher symbols]

Return immediately.

Wiggins nodded, even though he couldn't make out the words. "Who do you think it is?"

"To create and decode these ciphers, one needs to know how to read and write. Who in the gang has that ability, Wiggins?"

Meanwhile, back at the Castle, Pilar had been wielding a broom for over an hour. The area around the fire pit was finally clean. Most of the debris had been picked up, crated, or carried out to the alley.

"It will be cold sleepin' without a blanket again," said Pete.

"I'm gonna miss my old pillow," said Simpson.

Alfie sighed. "I'm gonna miss the Grand Dame. I can't play highwayman no more."

"Listen to you," said Alistair. "You didn't have any of this when you was on the streets. You've all gone soft. I've heard enough of this sissy talk." He crossed the carriage factory and stormed through the newly repaired trapdoor.

Pilar felt a tingling sensation in her hands as she watched him leave, and she knew enough to trust it. Handing the broom to Alfie, she said, "Finish up. I'll be back."

"Other than you and Pilar, Oz, none of us can read."

"Wiggins, someone can. The first three messages were written by someone in the gang."

Wiggins thought. "Well, Rohan is tryin' to teach himself."

Ozzie considered this. "Unless he's made significant progress since I left, it couldn't be him."

"How do you know it's one of us? It could be anyone."

"Wiggins, Master only gave directions to *us*."

"What about Billy? He hears everything that goes on in Master's flat."

"You said Billy wasn't in the flat when Master instructed you to go to the cemetery."

"Elliot?" Wiggins looked confused and unsure.

"I don't think so. He wasn't around when we received the assignment to go to the Tower of London, and besides, I'm certain he can't read."

Wiggins smacked himself on the side of the head as he realized who Ozzie had been thinking of all along.

"I can't believe it, Oz. He's my oldest mate. He wouldn't . . ."

Ozzie stood up. "He must have learned a lot in the workhouse."

CHAPTER NINETEEN

CAPTURED AGAIN!

The clop of horse hooves smacking the cobble-stones filled the air. Pilar watched Alistair jump on the back of a carriage heading toward the Thames. Like a doe, she sprung onto the back of another going in the same direction. Ozzie and Wiggins came around the corner just in time to glimpse them. With no other carriages immediately nearby, the boys followed on foot.

Carts, hansoms, hackneys, and a few broughams vied for passage on the street. When Pilar's carriage caught up to Alistair's, she stole a furtive glance at him before curling back under her cloak to hide.

Meanwhile, street traffic increased, giving Ozzie and Wiggins an opportunity to gain ground. But the exertion left them panting and light-headed. They were relieved to at last board a carriage.

Seeing Pilar dismount at the foot of Lambeth Bridge, the boys did the same.

"Alistair jumped off a few streets back, and now he's crossing the bridge over the Thames." Pilar pointed him out to Ozzie and Wiggins. They watched him for a moment — allowing a distance to clear between them — and then followed.

"*La mofeta!*" Pilar stormed. "I knew he was a skunk the first time I saw him."

"I still ain't sure . . ." Wiggins kept his gaze on the ground.

"If you don't believe he's guilty, why are you here?" Pilar snapped.

"We shall soon see the truth of the matter," Ozzie said to defuse the tension as the three crossed the bridge and tracked Alistair along the riverbank.

"He is walking with purpose and a familiarity of the area," Pilar noted.

Ozzie had been thinking the same thing.

But Wiggins kept quiet. He knew better than to engage with Pilar when she was so heated. And besides, part of him worried that she was right.

Alistair turned onto a mucky path, and so did they, past shacks, tenements, and factories, where the air was heavy with the rotten-egg smell of sulfur. Covering their mouths, they passed through a viaduct onto a street with a brightly painted building and a red-and-white sign announcing, JENNIE'S GIN SHOP. Alistair went inside.

Wiggins approached the window and peered in. He stayed there longer than was safe, the truth registering like an arrow in his gut.

His oldest friend had betrayed him.

At last, Ozzie pried him away from the window.

"You were right," Wiggins said foggily. "Alistair is in there with the duke and his mates."

Before Ozzie or Pilar had a chance to respond,

the door swung open. The three dashed around the side of the building as Alistair, the duke, and another Gent exited.

When they passed, Ozzie placed a hand on Wiggins's shoulder. "Are you all right?"

He nodded.

"Then let's go," Ozzie said. "We have a case to solve."

They followed Alistair and the Gents down a muddy path and past a row of shacks before turning onto a wide dirt road. A tall brick wall lined one side, and railway tracks the other. Smokestacks puffed sooty clouds into the early evening sky, darkening it even more.

At the water's edge, the Gents boarded a small barge, tied to an old wooden dock. With no windows or light emanating from within, it resembled a large black coffin, floating grimly on the water.

Wiggins waved Ozzie and Pilar behind some old crates stacked near the dock. They crouched, waited, and watched. Sounds in the brush popped around them, but no one passed.

Wiggins thought about Alistair. How could his oldest mate betray him? What did the duke have to offer that Wiggins didn't?

"What should we do?" asked Pilar.

"Take a closer look," said Ozzie.

Absently, Wiggins nodded his agreement.

Ozzie motioned for the others to wait as he started slowly down the dock. Just as he reached the barge, a Gent appeared on deck and grabbed him.

"Get inside, runt!" The Gent pointed at the barge.

Reluctantly, Ozzie climbed down. He hoped that Wiggins and Pilar would get help swiftly.

A large square hatch opened on the deck. Lantern light radiated from inside. Ozzie stepped down through the hatch into the barge. As he did, he watched grimly as Wiggins and Pilar were dragged down the dock by two other Gents.

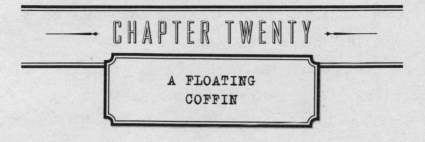

CHAPTER TWENTY

A FLOATING COFFIN

A thick rope bound Ozzie, Wiggins, and Pilar together around their waists, arms pinned to their sides.

Searching for an exit, Ozzie's gaze darted about. A few oil lamps illuminated the long, rectangular space. A dozen hammocks hung at one end. In the center, a large table sat littered with dirty papers and empty bottles.

Four Gents hovered over them. The duke rested one hand on Alistair's shoulder and gestured with the other. "Yous thought yous was clever escapin' from that crypt. But I knew I'd be seein' yous again."

Wiggins stared at Alistair.

The duke bent down and turned Wiggins's face to his. "Last time I was nice 'cause we needed somethin'. Yous got nothin' we need now. Yous know what that means, don't yous?"

"No, I don't, you ape, but I guess you're goin' to tell me." Wiggins strained in his ropes.

The duke grabbed Wiggins by the hair and yanked his head to the side. "Don't be *cheeky* with me. That's it, boys and girls, yous are done. Just like the dirty little factory yous all live in."

Wiggins turned to look at his old friend. "Are we done, Al?"

Alistair held his gaze. "These are my mates now, Wiggins. The duke helped me get out of the workhouse. You did nothin' for me. You didn't even try. They are a whole different class from you and the Irregulars. And now I am, too."

"The only reason he got you out, mate, was so you could spy on us. That's your new friend, someone who is usin' you," Wiggins said sadly.

"*Mofeta. Me diste mala espina desde el primer momento en que te vi,*" Pilar growled. "Skunk. I knew you looked shady the first time I saw you."

Alistair lunged at her, but the duke held him back.

"The girl has enough problems now because she keeps poor company. A shame really." The duke stared unctuously at Pilar. Then he snapped his fingers.

"Gents! We must meet the others. Leave nothin' behind."

The three boys came to attention, adjusted their hats, and took their last swallows from the bottles they were holding.

"Do you think the professor is going to do something special for you?" said Ozzie. "He will make you dig at the site like poor laborers, searching for *his* treasure. He'll pay you little, and those fine suits will be ruined from dust."

The duke grabbed Ozzie by the collar, but then took control of himself. "*Shirty*, are we? Yous think yous know somethin', runt? Well, maybe. But it won't help none 'cause you'll never be able to share it with Sherlock Holmes, or no one else." He smirked as he tossed an oil lamp on the floor not twenty feet away from Ozzie.

The glass shattered and flames spilled out across the floor, spreading swiftly and lapping up the walls.

"Enjoy the evenin'." The duke pulled himself up through the hatch.

One by one, the three other Gents and Alistair followed. Alistair took one last look at Wiggins as smoke filled the barge. "Sorry, mate."

As soon as they were gone, Ozzie ordered, "We need to all push back against one another and try to stand!" When he gave the command, they braced their legs, which were not tied, and rose together.

Heat and smoke crept closer. Ozzie and Pilar started coughing. "What now?" she managed.

Ozzie looked at the hatch. "We can't climb out tied together. We have to cut these ropes."

"How?" Wiggins started coughing, too. Flames licked the floor just a few feet away.

As a unit, they stumbled back, gasping for breath, their eyes burning from the smoke.

"Find something we can rub up against." But even as Ozzie said it, he could see there was nothing that would help.

"I can't breathe. I have to sit down." Pilar started to cry.

The three inched as far away from the flames as they could and then sunk to the floor.

Was it all going to end here, Pilar wondered, in this floating coffin?

Just then, footsteps sounded on the deck above them. A shadowy figure slid down the hatch.

Through squinted, watery eyes, Wiggins saw the figure pull out a knife. Was the duke going to mercifully finish them off before the flames got them? Or had Alistair changed his mind and come to rescue them?

"Out now!" a familiar voice shouted, pushing each of them up the hatch and onto the dock just as the flames swallowed the barge.

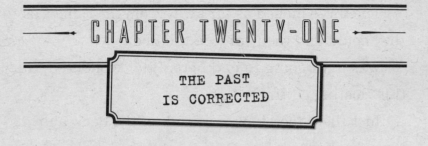

CHAPTER TWENTY-ONE

THE PAST
IS CORRECTED

Dark smudges of dirt and oil covered Elliot's face. His red hair glowed in the moonlight. "Fire's a wicked thing," he said as the four collapsed on the dock and watched the barge burn. "I know it better than most. It took my family, and I curse it every day."

Still wheezing, Ozzie looked incredulously at Elliot.

Pilar wiped hot tears from her cheeks. "Thank you for saving us. We would have died down there."

Elliot nodded solemnly.

Wiggins rubbed his stinging eyes. "Where did you come from?"

"I been followin' them Gents since the cemetery. I saw 'em go into that chapel after you. I heard 'em talkin', and they knew you was there. Like someone told 'em." Elliot paused and looked at Wiggins. "I knew right off who was 'elpin' 'em. I knew from the past, if you get me."

Wiggins felt a wave of understanding wash over him, and was ashamed of how he had been treating Elliot. He'd made a mistake long ago about who was his true friend.

Leading them down the dock, away from the water, Elliot continued, "When they came up out of the catacombs, I wanted to go for you, but decided to follow 'em instead. I am glad I did, 'cause now I know where the temple is."

"The temple?" asked Pilar.

"The temple of the goddess. The temple that Professor Moriarty is diggin' up."

"You saw Moriarty!?" they all said at once.

"I think it was 'im. They kept callin' 'im Professor, anyway."

"Have you seen the temple?" asked Ozzie.

"No," said Elliot, "I just heard 'em talkin' 'bout it and seen 'em diggin'."

"Where is the dig?" asked Pilar.

"On the other side of the river, near an old tube station. Just down the stairs and through the tunnel — like it's been waitin' for us."

"Can you take us there?" asked Wiggins.

Elliot nodded and led them to a street where a few tired hackney cabs waited. They all pooled their money and negotiated a ride across the river.

"Mark Lane Station," Elliot told the driver.

"How did you know that Alistair worked with the Gents?" Pilar asked as the hackney lurched forward, pulling them through the dark streets of Lambeth.

"Someone must've told those Gents you were down in the catacombs. I knew it wasn't one of the boys. We all been together too long. But Alistair just showed up and got right into the case. It didn't seem natural."

Ozzie observed Elliot in a new light. The boy had some smarts about him.

"That and there was that time, Wiggins, you remember, over a year ago. We hadn't eaten in days and were so hungry our bellies hurt. You, Alistair, and me went marketin'. We had that plan about pinchin' some food."

"I do remember," said Wiggins. "We were desperate."

"That's right, and we went to the marketplace and the plan was you would take a piece of cheese off a stand and when the monger went to chase you and left the stand unguarded, Alistair and me would take whatever we could get."

Wiggins nodded.

"And later, back at the Castle, Alistair told all of you that I must've eaten most of the food on the way back and that's why I didn't have much with me." Elliot's voice sounded a bit wobbly in the dark of the carriage. "And Alistair said that I shouldn't get nothin' to eat 'cause I already had me fill, and you all listened to 'im, even when I tried to tell the truth of what happened."

Wiggins remembered it well. Elliot had denied eating the cheese to the point at which tears welled up in his eyes. But he smelled like cheese, and he looked guilty, and Alistair was different then, reliable. Elliot wasn't.

"I didn't eat nothin', it was 'im. I saw how much he took off that cart and when we got back to the Castle, I saw how little he had. I didn't grab as much as 'im 'cause he grabbed first, and by the time I was loadin' up, another monger came runnin' after us. You all blamed me, and I never got one bite of nothin' that night. All 'cause Alistair lied and cheated. If I'd had a place to go, I would've left the gang that night. I still might have gone, but it wasn't much after that Alistair got caught stealin' and went to the workhouse. I thought that was that."

They all sat in silence. Pilar wanted to take Elliot's hand or offer him some support, but she realized they didn't have that closeness so she just nodded sympathetically.

Ozzie thought he understood Elliot now. The months of finding him so disagreeable melted away.

Wiggins cleared his throat. "I am sorry, Stitch, I made a big mistake. I guess we all did."

"Well, at least you believe me now," said Elliot. "All right, enough of the past," he said as he gazed out the window.

"Right," said Wiggins, thinking again of Alistair and wishing he could let it go as easily.

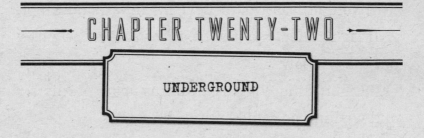

CHAPTER TWENTY-TWO

UNDERGROUND

As the hackney pulled up to the Mark Lane Station, the gang spied one of the Gents go down the underground stairs. They waited a few minutes and then followed. But they had no coins left to pay for entry.

"Earlier, I ran by when no one was lookin'. With four of us, that won't be easy." Elliot observed the station attendant.

"I have an idea," said Ozzie, looking at Pilar. "But it means you'll have to catch up with us."

At the ticket booth, Pilar rocked on her feet. Her eyes traveled up into her head. She brought the back of her hand to her forehead, moaned, and then dropped to the ground.

Everyone in the station, including the attendant, stopped and stared. An elderly woman and a few men bent down to help her. One of the men fanned her with a newspaper.

"She's fainted clear away," the elderly woman said, touching Pilar's cheeks.

Meanwhile, the boys slipped swiftly and inconspicuously past the ticket booth and down the stairs to the platform.

"I believe I'm all right," Pilar said, opening her eyes. "What time is it? I mustn't be late to Granny's."

The elderly woman helped her to her feet, then kindly paid for her ticket and accompanied her down the stairs. "Take your time, dearie," she said.

Pilar nodded as she stole a glance at the boys, heading for the far end of the platform. Like rats, they scurried down onto the tracks and disappeared into the darkness of the tunnel.

Pilar worried less about their safety and more that they might go on without her. The platform vibrated from the rumble of an approaching train. When it stopped in front of her, the elderly woman squeezed Pilar's hand. "Come, dearie."

"Thank you," Pilar said, and then, much to the woman's surprise, turned and ran down the platform, where she waited for the train to pull away. As soon as it did, Pilar jumped down onto the track. The boys were waiting for her in a side alcove.

"That was a fine bit of actin'," said Elliot. "You would've made Mr. Holmes proud."

Pilar grinned a self-satisfied grin in Wiggins's direction. "I'm glad you and Ozzie are back. We need your smarts."

Ozzie listened in the dark for any movement or sound. Sensing nothing, he said, "Let's go."

Elliot led the way as they picked through the darkness. A short time later, they arrived at an abandoned station platform. In tile on the wall, it said TOWER HILL.

Elliot stopped. "We're almost there. Just past this station is a passage that leads to where they are diggin'."

"One of us should go for Master," said Wiggins, looking at Pilar. "If this is the spot, he needs to know right away."

Ozzie agreed it was a good plan.

Pilar crossed her arms. "I am not leaving."

"And I need to show you the way," Elliot said.

Wiggins and Ozzie looked at each other.

"All right, then," Wiggins agreed. "Let's go a little farther."

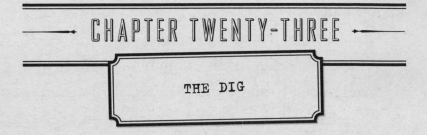

CHAPTER TWENTY-THREE

THE DIG

Overhead air shafts lit the way through a large tunnel. The air was thick and dusty and pressed uncomfortably on Ozzie's chest.

"We have been spending too much time underground for my liking," he said, reaching inside his coat for his cod liver oil. He took a swig.

"When the case is over, we'll ask Master for a change of scenery," Wiggins assured him.

A loud noise, like a train engine, pierced the quiet. Cautiously, they followed the sound into a cavern. At the far end, about a quarter mile away, stood a small hill. As the gang drew closer — stopping and crouching now and again to be certain they were alone — they discovered the hill was actually a towering mound of freshly dug dirt and stone, climbing some thirty feet high.

They could have circled around it, but Elliot led them straight up. He dropped onto all fours and crawled to manage the steep incline. The others followed. The climb was difficult, for the dirt would sometimes give way, causing them to slide backward.

At the top, they lay on their stomachs and peered down. Below, large lanterns illuminated a vast excavation site. A beastly-looking machine on rotating tracks blew smoke and hissed. A train engine made up its body, a giant shovel, its head and neck. Scooping dirt and stone, it unearthed a series of two-story stone archways. Ozzie covered his ears and said, "It's a steam shovel."

Approximately twenty-five men, including at least a dozen Gents, wielded shovels, picks, and brooms to clear away dirt from inside the archways. Their speed and proficiency reminded Wiggins of the colony of carpenter ants that invaded the carriage factory every spring.

Scaffolding had been erected so that work occurred on both the upper and lower levels of the archways. The duke chipped away at one with a large miner's pick. The Gent who'd trapped Ozzie on the barge swept away the debris. But none of the archways had yet been cleared of enough sediment to allow passage.

Meanwhile, Alistair walked from worker to worker, carrying a pail of water and a ladle with which to quench the thirsty. Wiggins's chest burned at the sight of him.

Pilar recognized the design of the stone archways immediately. It was identical to the ones they'd seen at the Tower of London and in the catacombs of Norwood Cemetery.

Ozzie had made the same connection as he watched the excavation in awe. The sheer number of archways and their prodigious height transported him to ancient Rome, the setting of so many stories his grandfather had once read to him. Those lazy Sunday afternoons with Grandfather, and all that had happened in the intervening years, felt like a lifetime ago, or perhaps like someone else's lifetime.

Ozzie forced himself to shake off the memory and concentrate on the workers. His gaze traveled from one to the next, finally landing on him. Even from far away, his tall, thin frame and domed forehead were unmistakable. Though Ozzie had met him face-to-face before, suddenly, looking down on England's greatest criminal mind made his heart race. In his black cape and top hat, Professor Moriarty lorded over the dig like Cerberus over the gate to Hades.

Another man, wearing spectacles, a tweed vest, and a dusty straw hat stood beside him.

Ozzie motioned to the others to inch back down the dirt mound, out of sight.

"Is the man in the top hat who I think he is?" asked Pilar.

Ozzie nodded.

Wiggins grabbed his hair. "The Napoleon of Crime is down there, and we're alone with him and all those men?!"

Elliot put a hand on his shoulder. "Easy, mate."

Wiggins looked around and, in a quieter voice, said, "Okay, no more messin' around. We know where Moriarty is and what he is doin' and where the darn temple is most likely. We need to go tell Master. Our job is done."

Pilar peeked over the top of the mound. "We can't leave yet. We need to stop him."

"Stop Moriarty?" Wiggins exclaimed. "Master is always tellin' us to observe and report back and not to take risks. We ain't always listened to 'im, but I think it's time we start."

The steam shovel grew louder and they strained to hear one another over the din.

Pilar looked to Ozzie. "But what if Moriarty gets away?"

"Wiggins is right. Someone must report to Master. One or two of us can stay. If Moriarty leaves, we'll follow him. The temple site is not going anywhere so —"

Before Ozzie could finish his thought, the steam shovel dumped a full load onto the mound. Stone and dirt rained down upon them.

Wiggins and Pilar scrambled to their feet and ran through the pelting rubble. Behind them, Elliot rolled like a log down the back side of the mound. Ozzie stood to follow, but slipped and tumbled down the front side. He came to rest at the feet of two enormous men wielding shovels. One man dropped his shovel and hoisted Ozzie to his feet. The other dragged him away.

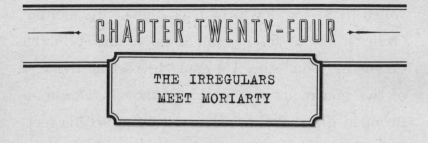

The steam shovel had stopped digging and its driver climbed out. Though less clamorous, the machine still puffed and hissed like some ancient beast. A group of workers, including the duke and Alistair, surrounded Ozzie.

One of the men laughed and asked the steam shovel operator, "What kinda treasure you dig up, Mick?"

Moriarty glared at Ozzie as he directed his men, "Go see if there are others."

"This one's one of Holmes's boys," said the duke. "I don't know how he made it 'ere. We left 'im in Lambeth. He should be burnt up and sunk to the bottom of the river by now."

"He's here because he followed you," Moriarty said disgustedly. "Clearly, he is more capable than you and your boys."

The duke's broad shoulders slumped. A few of the Gents shot looks of concern at one another.

Moriarty turned to Ozzie. "Tell me, boy, do you have friends with you?"

The pressure inside Ozzie's chest was unbearable. He reached inside his coat for his tonic, but as soon as he did, Moriarty swatted it out of his hand. The bottle shattered on the ground, the precious cod liver oil soaking into the dirt. Ozzie stared at it and felt his lungs seize up even more.

"Answer me, boy!"

"They were here . . ." Ozzie managed, "but I sent them for Mr. Holmes."

"I see," said Moriarty, rubbing his immense forehead. Then he ordered his men back to work. The man in the straw hat remained beside him. Moriarty pointed to the duke. "You stay with us and our little friend here.

"Carter," Moriarty said to the man in the straw hat, "we need to focus our energies on a single archway. The second story will have less sediment. Organize the men. If we don't gain access quickly, we will have to use less subtle means." He pointed to the steam shovel.

"What about Sherlock Holmes?" asked Carter.

"If Holmes knew our whereabouts, he would be here already. He's immersed in the search for his friend, Dr. Watson, a very *opportune* mishap for us. We will be done here long before Holmes solves that case and turns to this one."

"What about the lad's friends? They could be warning him as we speak."

Moriarty turned to Ozzie. "You were merely bluffing when you said you sent your mates for Holmes, were you not?"

Ozzie said nothing.

The duke grabbed his arm and twisted until Ozzie's whole body shuddered with pain. He bit his lip to keep from crying out.

"Speak, runt!" the duke demanded.

Just then, the men Moriarty had sent searching returned with Pilar, Wiggins, and Elliot.

"We found 'em headin' for the station," said one.

The duke shoved Ozzie to the ground.

Moriarty fixed the duke with a hard stare. "We have no time for these distractions. I do not enjoy being followed by Holmes's urchins. Serve me better, Dickie. Now tie them up. We will do away with them later."

Before he turned to go, Moriarty studied Ozzie one more time. "You look familiar, boy. I know I have seen you previously."

Ozzie remained silent.

Moriarty's reptilian eyes bore into him. "Infuriating. Just like your master." Moriarty paced away.

The duke had fire in his eyes as he lifted Ozzie off the ground like a rag doll and thrust him forward. Other men pushed Wiggins, Pilar, and Elliot along.

"We are all going to have a talk," the duke growled.

"Okay, Dickie," Wiggins mocked, before he received a swift kick to his leg.

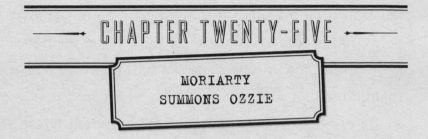

CHAPTER TWENTY-FIVE

MORIARTY
SUMMONS OZZIE

Ozzie, Wiggins, Pilar, and Elliot were deposited on the ground near a toolbox, like discarded pieces of wood.

"Well, at least we're not all tied up to each other this time," Wiggins said, trying to lighten the mood.

"Yes, this is much more comfortable," said Pilar, groaning.

Elliot twisted in the ropes bound around his wrists. "Bloody Gents."

Alistair passed them, sheepishly carting his bucket of water.

"Hey, Al," Wiggins called. "Have you a drink for your old mate? Sure could 'ave used it on that burnin' barge."

Alistair kept walking, his head down.

Ozzie watched the men on the scaffolding working tirelessly on two arches side by side. Removing the sediment from the archway was slow and tedious work. The sediment, a mixture of compacted dirt, stone, and clay looked hard as rock.

"Any ideas, Oz?" Wiggins said.

Ozzie considered the options and gazed over his shoulder into the deep toolbox. The tools inside it were out of reach, but the box itself was near enough. It had a sharp metal edge. Ozzie rubbed the rope against it. The other three watched. When one of the workmen looked over or passed, he would stop.

"What do you think they're goin' to do with us?" asked Pilar.

"As soon as they find the temple, they'll finish us," said Elliot.

Wiggins nodded. "Moriarty talks like a gentleman, but he ain't."

Grimly, the gang watched Moriarty and Carter standing some twenty feet away, observing the work. Occasionally, Moriarty gave Carter directions to pass on to the men. At one point, Moriarty pulled a small notebook from his pocket and paged through it.

"That must be Calico Finch's," said Pilar.

When two men yelled from the scaffolding, Carter ran over to investigate.

"The scrivener's apprentice."

Ozzie had been watching the action so intently that he was startled to see Moriarty's tall frame looming over him. His penetrating eyes held Ozzie like a magnet. He could not look away. But behind the snakelike ferocity, Ozzie sensed something else — familiarity, affection? Ozzie was trying to determine when Moriarty spoke again.

"You were apprenticed to Crumbly. His most elite forger. I remember you now. Does Sherlock Holmes know that you haven't always worked on the right side of the law?"

Moriarty remembered him? He thought him "elite"? Ozzie felt his cheeks burn, from pride or fear he could not tell.

Before he could respond, Carter appeared at Moriarty's side in an excited state.

"Professor, they forged a hole all the way through. In a few more hours, it should be large enough for us to enter!"

Moriarty addressed the man calmly, "How much time do you think we have, Carter? We are not doing an excavation for one of your esteemed benefactors. Scotland Yard could appear at any time. We need to send someone into that hole to see what is on the other side. If the Temple of Diana is there and not too close to those arches, we can use the steam shovel to break our way through."

"But Professor, those arches are architectural treasures —"

"They may be treasures," said Moriarty, "but they're of no value to me if they do not fit in my pocket. Finch's notes tell us that the temple may be filled with golden offerings. Treasure that can be carried away. Not even I can appropriate a temple or your valuable arches."

Carter's enthusiasm dissipated. "Professor, no one can fit through that hole. We need more time to enlarge it."

Moriarty's gaze returned to Ozzie. "There is one among us who can fit."

Ozzie perched on the scaffold with a rope tied tightly about his waist. The duke held the other end like a leash. Moriarty and Carter stood beside them.

"You understand your orders?" Moriarty asked.

Ozzie nodded.

"There may not be much air in the chamber on the other side, so proceed with care," said Carter.

Moriarty gave Ozzie a thoughtful look. "You were nearly of use to me once, but my plans then were thwarted. Do not disappoint me this time, boy. We are not often given second chances."

Ozzie nodded again as the duke thrust a lantern into his hand. Ozzie looked across to his friends who were still tied near the toolbox.

"If you try to further disrupt our plans," Moriarty warned, "your friends will bear the burden of your decision." Then he placed a hand on

Ozzie's shoulder and in a softer tone said, "I know you can do it, my boy."

Ozzie held the lantern in front of him and peered into the hole. A tube approximately five or six feet long and fourteen inches wide had been burrowed through the sediment.

He glanced from Moriarty to his friends. Then, without a word, he squeezed himself into the tunnel.

CHAPTER TWENTY-SIX

OZZIE MEETS DIANA

The narrow space was dark and suffocating. Ozzie felt queasy as he snaked through, propelling himself forward with his right hand and holding the lantern in front of him with his left. The rough surface scraped his arms, stomach, and legs. There was a dull pressure inside his head, and his thoughts would not align properly — as though his brain were filled with sand.

Would he be able to find the treasure and keep his friends from harm? Moriarty said that he would do away with him and the others once he got his gold. But seeing him up close, Ozzie couldn't tell if he meant it. Where was Master? And why had he lied to the Irregulars? Recalling his conversation with him earlier that day, Ozzie felt sick. Would he even want such a cold, detached man for a father?

His breathing grew labored as though something clutched him around the throat. He was about to reach for his tonic, but remembered it was gone. The thought made his throat constrict more. He tried to swallow and couldn't. His head pounded, his vision blurred, and his hands sweated. As a faint began to overtake him, he willed himself against it. Somehow, he reached the other side. Hanging his head out into open space, Ozzie gulped air.

He yanked the rope, signaling the duke to pull it taut and let it out slowly with each subsequent tug. Breathing more steadily, Ozzie slid out of the opening and was lowered. He continued to take deep breaths, testing that there was sufficient air. Sooner than expected, he hit the ground with a thud.

He found himself in a small courtyard, enclosed by stone archways. Columns lay on the ground like fallen trees. A large stone pedestal stood before him. It was chiseled with writing in a language he could not read. At his feet was the disembodied head of a marble horse.

Ozzie kicked the thick dust and discovered a mosaic-tiled floor in browns and greens. He kicked more and, suddenly, a woman's face appeared. Her almond-shaped eyes stared up at him, transporting him back centuries.

Moriarty and his men stood anxiously on the scaffolding, waiting for Ozzie's return. Wiggins had been rubbing the rope against the toolbox since Ozzie left. Finally, it had begun to fray.

Pilar cleared her throat. When Wiggins looked up, one of the workmen was standing over them.

"You're in my way. I need to reach those tools."

The man was stocky and bearded with a significant paunch that strained the buttons of his dusty striped work shirt. He bent down to reach into the toolbox, but then turned, pulled a knife from his belt, and sliced the ropes that bound Wiggins's wrists and ankles.

"Keep your hands behind you and don't move your legs or they might notice you are free. I'll drop the knife behind you so you can release the others at the right time."

"Master?" Wiggins whispered.

"There is no time for conversation," Holmes said, rummaging through the toolbox. "I don't know how you discovered this place on your own, or how many times I have warned you against such perilous acts." Holmes picked up a large hammer and pretended to study it. "Pilar, if Moriarty were facing us, would you be able to read his lips?"

Pilar was still registering that the stout man before her was Holmes. "Yes, I think so."

"Good," Holmes said, standing. "If he summons the steam shovel, that is your signal to flee. Return the way you came."

"But, Master —"

Holmes turned and abruptly strode away before Wiggins could finish his question.

*　　*　　*

Ozzie's lantern pierced the darkness as he continued walking. He came upon the temple — five stone steps led to a circle of eight columns, capped by a dome. The structure appeared intact, frozen in time, as if it had waited there for over a millennium for Ozzie to discover it. He tugged the rope for slack and entered.

The floor was made of smooth marble, the ceiling carved with animals frozen in mid-leap. Ozzie's gaze traveled all around and finally settled on *her*. She stood nearly ten feet tall and looked down upon him almost regally from her pedestal. She wore the clothes of a huntress and carried a bow and a quiver of arrows. Her eyes, both strong and gentle, utterly transfixed him. He understood immediately why Calico Finch had been obsessed with her. She was magnificent.

"Diana," he breathed.

He reached up and touched her foot. It felt gritty. When he removed his hand, he saw that his fingerprints had left golden impressions in the dust. Brushing away more dust, he discovered that she was made of solid gold.

He stood in silent awe for a moment longer before finishing his circle.

At the back of the temple, he found a marble altar framed by two large marble boxes. As he drew closer, he could see that coins were scattered across the altar and overflowed from the boxes. He picked one up. The gold disc was cool and weighty. The front bore the image of a curly-haired man in profile.

Ozzie could hardly believe that he was standing amidst the ancient goddess, the temple, and the casks of gold — a treasure that Moriarty was willing to kill for. Ozzie felt his heart race with exhilaration, or was it fear? Did he want to be assisting Moriarty? And what might all of this mean for Ozzie, and for his friends?

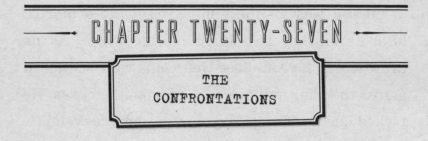

CHAPTER TWENTY-SEVEN

THE CONFRONTATIONS

Wiggins, Pilar, and Elliot watched as Ozzie was reeled back out of the hole and onto the scaffolding. He raised his right hand and held the gold coin aloft. The workmen cheered at the sight of it. Moriarty plucked it from Ozzie's hand and examined it.

"He is asking Ozzie where it came from," Pilar told Wiggins and Elliot. "Ozzie is saying he found it in the temple and that there are more, many more. Moriarty is praising his work. Now he's asking Ozzie how far the temple was from the wall of arches. Ozzie says about thirty feet. Moriarty is directing the men to start up the steam shovel. That's our cue."

"The steam shovel is next to us," Elliot said. "They are all looking in our direction. How is Wiggins supposed to cut us loose without anyone seeing?"

Before Wiggins could answer, the stocky workman walked up to the steam shovel and climbed into its compartment. Of course Master had a plan. He started the engine. The steam and hiss heightened like a dragon awakening. Holmes drove it slowly backward on its treads and then turned it toward the scaffolding. As the steam shovel moved, it blocked the workmen's view of the gang.

"Brilliant!" Wiggins said as he reached for the knife and cut Pilar and Elliot free. When the two paused to see what Holmes would do next, Wiggins demanded, "Listen to Master and run out of 'ere. When you're back on the street, stop the first policeman you see and bring 'elp. Now go!"

Pilar hesitated. "What about you?"

"After I get Oz, we'll join you," Wiggins assured her.

Pilar and Elliot ran around the far side of the mound and disappeared. Wiggins crept to the rear of the steam shovel and stealthily climbed up into the driver's compartment.

"I sent the others to get 'elp," he told Holmes, as he crouched down so as not to be seen.

Holmes shot him a disapproving look before shifting levers and directing the steam shovel straight at the wall of arches. "You should have gone with them, Wiggins. This will be dangerous."

Meanwhile, Moriarty directed Ozzie to explain to Carter the layout of the temple and its courtyard. Ozzie went into every detail, the mosaics, the golden statue of Diana, and the casks of gold coins. He described the location of the temple in relation to the wall of arches and the safest place to break through the wall without damaging the temple. He spoke excitedly, almost uncontrollably. He felt a rush of pride and discomfort. Had he said too much?

Moriarty and Carter were jubilant.

"You have a sharp eye for detail, boy, and a certain thoughtfulness I find unusual for someone of your age and circumstances. When this is over, and I am the wealthiest man in all of England, I believe we need to discuss your future." Moriarty patted Ozzie on the shoulder. His touch was strangely affectionate. Ozzie felt himself leaning into it and then recoiling. It's Moriarty, he reminded himself, England's most dangerous criminal.

When Ozzie looked up, he saw the dejected expressions of the duke and several Gents, including Alistair, who appeared deflated and ineffectual sitting on the edge of his water bucket. Sweaty and covered with dirt from their labors, the rival gang did not seem impressive or even very threatening.

Carter jumped down from the scaffold and directed the steam shovel toward the area Ozzie had suggested.

Everyone's attention shifted to the machine, except Ozzie's. He noticed that his friends were no longer tied up. Ozzie had found the temple *and* delivered the coin, as instructed. Had Moriarty done away with them anyway?

Carter removed his hat and waved the driver

forward. With the shovel arm extended to its full height, the machine bore down on the wall. Carter motioned again with his hat, this time for the driver to retract the shovel. But it plowed ahead, just missing him as he dove out of the way.

Moriarty, Ozzie, the workmen, and the Gents looked on from the scaffold as the steam shovel chugged toward them. Before they could react, the shovel slammed down on the scaffold with full force, splintering its planks and collapsing nearly the entire structure.

Ozzie managed to grab hold of a support pole that had withstood the impact. Grasping the pole with his arms and legs and suspended some twenty feet in the air, he teetered in one direction and tottered in another. He had seen Moriarty swing to the ground with surprising agility just before the shovel hit, but he could not see where he went. Ozzie was now trying to pick a good time to jump.

Poles, tools, and workers rained down on the ground. Some men hollered while others lay crushed. Some ran for cover while others were dragged out of the shovel's path.

As it lurched forward again, Ozzie saw Wiggins waving to him from the steam shovel. He held his breath and jumped down onto the roof of the driver's compartment.

Inside, Holmes shifted gears and pursued the workmen. Wiggins saw the duke and a few others jump out of their path. Before they knew it, the duke had climbed up into the doorway of the compartment and swung a large wrench at Wiggins. Wiggins stepped aside as the wrench hit the wall with a clang. The duke swung at him again. Wiggins ducked, and then, with all his might, rammed him with his shoulder. The duke flew from the compartment and landed with a thud on a bed of excavated boulders. Holmes, who still had control of the steam shovel, yelled, "Well done, my boy!"

Just then, Pilar and Elliot led Watson and Inspector Lestrade around the dirt mound. The sound of policemen's whistles echoed throughout the cavern as uniformed officers flooded inside. They rounded up the workmen and the Gents. Lestrade managed to grab Carter.

Nowhere in the melee did Ozzie see Moriarty. He turned to consider the jagged wall of the cavern. At first, he saw nothing, just the stone wall that jutted up some forty feet to the ceiling. But then, a flicker of light sparked along the wall. Ozzie jumped down from the steam shovel and followed it.

From inside the driver's compartment, Wiggins saw it all. He climbed out and pursued Ozzie.

"Wiggins, wait!" Holmes called to him.

But Wiggins ran off.

From a distance, the entrance to the tunnel was hidden by the jagged rock. As Ozzie approached, he observed a hazy glow emanating from within and followed it. The tunnel zigzagged, but Ozzie moved swiftly, nearly tripping over a top hat that lay on the ground. The dull pressure was still in his head. He did not know what he would do if he caught up with Moriarty. He didn't know why he was chasing him. But he pressed on. When he came around a particularly sharp turn, Ozzie stopped abruptly.

There, resting on one knee, with a lantern in one hand and a revolver pointing straight at him in the other, was Moriarty.

"Why are you following me, boy?"

Ozzie strained for breath. "I don't know."

"Does anyone else know about this tunnel?"

"I don't think so."

"Are you tracking me or trying to leave with me?"

Ozzie wasn't sure. His brain felt dull and over-stuffed. His body throbbed with fatigue. "What did you mean about my future?" The words poured out without Ozzie even realizing he was saying them. He saw Moriarty's face relax. He saw his lips moving, but he couldn't hear anything. He watched Moriarty lower the revolver and reach for him. Ozzie's breath grew shorter and more labored as he took a step forward.

Images flashed across his mind: his mother's face in the tintypes; Great-aunt Agatha, sitting vacantly by the fire; Holmes in his flat, smoking his pipe and gazing out the window; Wiggins and Pilar; and then, his mother again, sick in bed and trying to tell him something just before she died.

"I think I want to leave," Ozzie managed before everything went black.

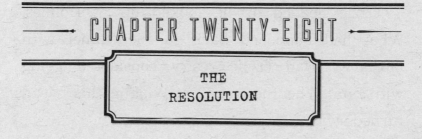

CHAPTER TWENTY-EIGHT

THE
RESOLUTION

Ozzie came to at the feet of Holmes, Wiggins, Pilar, and Elliot. Watson knelt beside him and assisted in sitting him up. His head ached.

They were back at the dig site, where most of the workmen were being led away by the police.

"I'm glad to see you have joined us again, Osgood," Holmes said matter-of-factly. "Watson, what is your diagnosis?"

"Fatigue. This lad needs a meal and a few days' rest." Watson patted him on the back.

"Wiggins tells me that you attempted to apprehend Moriarty on your own. I appreciate your commitment, Osgood, but next time, request our assistance, for few face Moriarty and survive. You are lucky Wiggins found you and carried you out of the tunnel."

Ozzie nodded as he looked up at Holmes. What had happened back in the tunnel with Moriarty? Had Ozzie really considered going with him? When he looked at Wiggins, his friend turned away.

"Once again, Irregulars, your services were exceptional," Holmes continued. "You helped to turn my friend Watson here into a fine diversion. Moriarty believed that Watson had been abducted and that we were searching for him, when in fact, all of my energies were focused on finding Moriarty and this site.

"I know that I deceived you by not sharing the ruse, but I suspected from the beginning that your acquaintance there" — Holmes motioned over to Alistair who was detained by one of the officers — "was an agent of Moriarty's.

"Despite my efforts to keep you in the dark, you still managed to discover Watson and Tuttle at the Tower of London. They were searching for the location of the Temple of Diana. Though we did not have the benefit of Calico Finch's journal, which directed Moriarty here, Tuttle reviewed the manuscripts that Finch had read the night of his murder. They provided some pieces to the puzzle but not the entire picture.

"Tuttle suspected a few possible locations for the Temple. The catacombs of the West Norwood Cemetery was one, the old Roman well at the Tower of London another. The riddle you brought me from the cemetery was meant to be found by you; it was Watson's way of indicating his next step.

"It was only through some understanding of the location of the ancient Roman structures on Tuttle's part and my contemporary knowledge of the excavations performed in this city, including my knowledge of the abandoned Tower Hill underground station and the auxiliary tunnels and chambers, that we ultimately arrived here.

"I had informed Lestrade of our suspicions and asked him to stand by."

"That's why he was waiting just outside when we reached the street?" said Pilar.

Holmes nodded.

"What I didn't expect is that you would find this site on your own."

"That was all Elliot," said Wiggins. "He followed them Gents all day without them knowin' it. Then he brought us 'ere."

Elliot flushed red in the cheeks and nodded.

"Fine work," said Holmes.

"Osgood, you are the only person in some fourteen hundred years to have gazed upon the treasure and the goddess Diana. What do you have to say?"

Ozzie looked up at Holmes. In spite of all that had happened, he still felt anxious to discuss their unfinished business. Realizing it would have to wait, he thrust his hands into his pockets and felt something. He pulled out the gold coin.

Holmes took it and examined it in awe. "A solid gold coin of a different millennium."

Wiggins shook his head and stormed away from the group. While the others admired the coin, Ozzie followed him.

"What's the matter, mate?" Ozzie asked.

"I tracked you, and I heard your talk with Moriarty. You were thinkin' 'bout goin' with 'im, weren't you?"

Ozzie felt stunned by the fact that Wiggins had witnessed everything and by his own behavior. He did not know which felt worse.

"Just before Moriarty left you, I saw 'im put that coin in your pocket. What's it all about, Oz? You thinkin' 'bout becomin' a crook? You goin' to betray me, too?" Wiggins's tone was harsh.

"No," Ozzie said weakly.

"Then why so chummy with 'im?"

Ozzie looked at the only true friend he had ever known. "Wiggins, without you and Pilar, I would be alone in the world. Today, this last year, has been confusing for me. Try to understand. I don't know what I meant to say to Moriarty or why he gave me that coin. All I know is that I don't want it. I don't want the coin, and I don't want to join him."

Wiggins tilted his head and considered his friend. His tired, sick, loyal friend. After a minute, he put an arm around Ozzie's shoulder and smiled. "You been a bit odd today, Oz, but I believe you. Now, let's not be too hasty about that coin, mate. We could be dinin' on roast beef tomorrow if we sell it to the museum."

Though weary, Ozzie perked up at Wiggins's change of heart.

"This is how I see it, Oz: We trade in that coin, and then we replace some of the damaged items in the Castle and 'ave a celebration."

"A celebration?" asked Ozzie.

Wiggins's eyes sparkled in the din of the cavern. "In honor of your return and a new start for the gang and . . ." Wiggins paused.

"What?" asked Ozzie.

"How 'bout Pilar becomin' an official Baker Street Irregular?"

The boys looked at her, eyes gleaming, as she proudly explained the events of the day to Holmes.

"Yes," Ozzie agreed. "That does sound like cause for celebration."

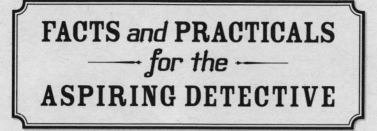

FACTS and PRACTICALS
— for the —
ASPIRING DETECTIVE

SLANG GLOSSARY

Twist and twirl: Girl (page 21)

These and those: Clothes (page 23)

Fal: Gal (page 24)

Rozzer: Police officer (page 28)

Plod: Police officer (page 29)

Blighter: Creep (page 36)

Neff off: Go away (page 38)

Pot of honey: Money (page 38)

Blimey: Oh, no (page 54)

Git: Stupid person (page 64)

Bugger off: Go away (page 66)

Bangers: Sausage (page 80)

Wally: Idiot (page 96)

Cheeky: Disrespectful (page 126)

Shirty: Smart-alecky (page 127)

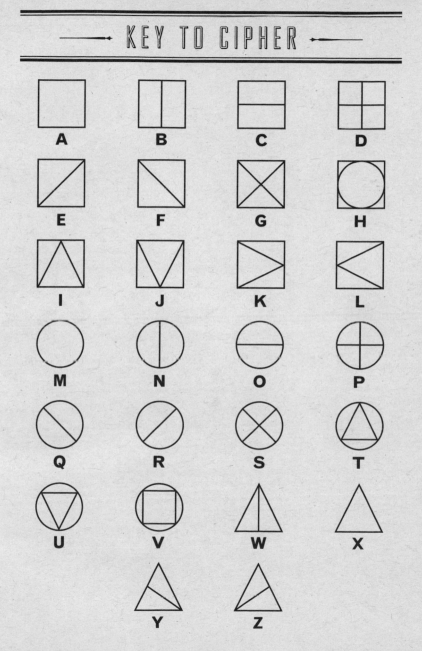

─TIPS FOR THE YOUNG CRYPTOLOGIST─

Secret messages of all kinds have existed for centuries, and the aspiring detective would be wise to familiarize himself with at least a few. The one Ozzie solves in this book is called a cipher. Ciphers are created by replacing each *letter* of a word with a symbol. They differ from codes, where *words* and *phrases* are replaced with symbols to represent each *word* or *phrase.*

The process of making a cipher is called encrypting. Someone who deciphers an encrypted message is called a cryptologist.

The experienced cryptologist employs certain tips to help in the process of deciphering, but there is also quite a bit of trial and error, as well.

Ciphers have always been part of Mr. Holmes's detective work. Note Sir Arthur Conan Doyle's story "The Adventure of the Dancing Men" (from which inspiration was drawn for *In Search of Watson*), where Holmes explains some basic points of cryptology:

As you are aware, E is the most common letter in the English alphabet and it predominates to so marked an extent that even in a short sentence one would expect to find it most often . . . [s]peaking roughly, T, A, O, I, N, S, H, R, D, and I are the numerical order in which the letters occur; but T, A, O and I are very nearly abreast of each other . . .

The renowned Sherlockian scholar Leslie S. Klinger offers a few additional pointers found in the Encyclopaedia Britannica (9th Ed. — a copy of which was kept on the bookshelves of Holmes's flat at 221B Baker Street):

All single letters must be *A*, *I* or *O*. Letters occurring together are *ee*, *oo*, *ff*, *ll*, *ss* . . . [t]he commonest words of two letters (roughly arranged in the order of their frequency) *of*, *to*, *in*, *it*, *is*, *be*, *he*, *by*, *or*, *as*, *at*, *an*, *so* . . . [t]he commonest words of three letters are *the* and *and* (in great excess), *for*, *are*, *but*, *all*, *not* . . .

Applying the above tips to the ciphers in this story (see page 116), you will notice that ⊿ appears in the four ciphers a total of twenty times, significantly more than any other symbol. Again drawing on the information above, we will assume then that it is an *e* (take a piece of tracing paper and place it over the page and write an *e* wherever that symbol appears in the ciphers).

You will also notice that periods appear after a series of letters, which might suggest that they signify the end of a word. Let's assume for a moment that this is true.

We can now see that there are eight three-letter

words, and that five of them end in *e*. Since we know that the most common three-letter words are *the* and *and*, we can see that five of the words are *the*. By deciphering these words, we know the symbols for *h* and *t* (a total of twenty-eight symbols in the four messages — again, using your tracing paper, write these letters over the appropriate symbols).

We also see that two of the three remaining three-letter words are identical and are most likely *and*, which give us the symbols for three more letters (*a*, *n*, and *d*) and a total of twenty-seven more symbols in the messages.

By paying attention to where double symbols appear, you will most likely pick up the double *oo* (in *Norwood*) and the double *ll* (in *alley*), and though you might not yet have deciphered *Norwood*, you probably have figured out the *y* in *alley*.

By now, you will surely recognize Mr. Holmes's name in the first cipher (which will also show you the symbol for *m* and *s*). The last word in the second cipher is obviously *cemetery* (giving you the symbols for *r* and *c*), and once you have that, the only letter you haven't deciphered in *catacombs* is a *b*. Using a little trial and error, you are at most minutes away from deciphering the rest.

Ciphers are fun to solve. They are also fun to create. Make up your own symbols and encrypt messages with your friends.

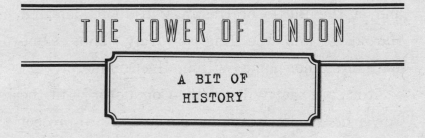

THE TOWER OF LONDON

A BIT OF HISTORY

Over nine hundred years after it was built, the Tower of London remains one of the most impressive structures in all of England. Serving at different times as a fortress, royal residence, jail, zoo, torture chamber, mint, observatory, vault, museum, and tourist attraction, the Tower has many a storied past.

Construction of the Tower began in 1078 at the direction of King William I. William was the Duke of Normandy and claimed title to the English crown after the death of the English King, Edward the Confessor. At the same time, Edward's brother, Harold Godwinson, also known as Harold II, himself claimed the throne of England, as did others. To press *his* claim, William invaded England, and at the Battle of Hastings in 1066, defeated Harold II and the English army. Thus came William's other name, William the Conqueror.

It is said that William the Conqueror built the Tower of London not only as a fortress to protect London from outside invaders, but also to protect himself from the Anglo-Saxon people he conquered.

The Tower of London was built in the eastern end of London, immediately adjacent to the Thames River and at the intersection of two old Roman walls.

Construction of the Tower took approximately twenty years and was not completed until after William's death.

The original portion of the Tower, known as the White Tower, is a tremendous building some ninety feet high with imposing stone walls that run anywhere from eleven to fifteen feet wide. Four turrets, three square and one round, appear on each corner of the walls. At the time it was completed around the year 1100, the Tower could be seen for miles around because of its size.

Over the next two centuries, additional fortifications were added to the Tower of London. A wall with thirteen towers was built around the White Tower. A second wall was also added. This one encircled the first and had another six towers. Around this last wall, a moat was dug which was fed by the River Thames.

In its beginning, the Tower was used primarily as a fortress and as a jail for important prisoners. Over the centuries, the Tower's prison played host to kings from Scotland and France; a Welsh prince; a number of English kings, queens, and princes; a saint; a president of the Continental Congress of colonial America; dukes; and miscellaneous noblemen. Among the prisoners were children, wives, brothers, and sisters of royalty. And some were even executed in the Tower's walls.

After a time, more comfortable lodgings were built within the Tower walls, and it became a home for several monarchs.

For centuries, a Royal Menagerie — a collection

of animals from England and around the world —
was kept at the Tower. Ultimately, the animals
were moved from the Tower, and the London Zoo
was started.

Other residents of the Tower include the Yeoman
Warders, who have guarded the buildings (and the
prisoners) for almost as long as the Tower's history.
Also known as Beefeaters, they wear traditional
uniforms based upon the uniform of the King's
Guard.

The Tower has also served as the home to the
Crown Jewels for over seven hundred years.

Lastly, at least six ravens have inhabited the
tower for centuries. Legend has it that if the ravens
ever leave the Tower, England will fall.

Today, the Tower of London is a popular tourist
site and has been so since Ozzie and the Irregulars
wandered the streets of London.

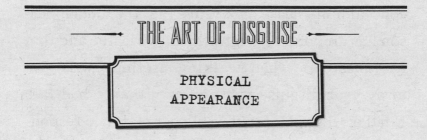

PHYSICAL APPEARANCE

The detective, at times, may need to appear different in size or shape from his given physique. Note how Sherlock Holmes, in this story, alters his tall, lean frame into that of a stout, burly workman. With a few tricks and the proper materials, you, too, can change your own size and shape.

Height Shoes of varying heel heights are invaluable. High boots can be hidden beneath long trousers, skirts, or dresses to create the illusion of a much taller person. A tall top hat for a gentleman or a high-plumed hat for a lady is another good trick for adding several inches. If you need to increase your height by more than a few inches,

193

you might enlist the help of a muscular friend and sit on his shoulders. Then, don a long outer coat to conceal him. Please make sure that the hidden person has air holes through which to breathe and that he takes care when walking. Nothing will give away your disguise more quickly than a bad fall. Further, the writer and publisher claim no responsibility for your recklessness, so if electing this technique, do proceed with caution.

Weight To increase your size, proper padding is essential. Soft foam (available at any good craft store) can be used to create the belly of a portly person. Likewise, this same material can be inserted into the shoulders of any jacket to give the impression of broad shoulders, or into the back side of trousers to create an ample bottom. A soft pillow or even a balloon may be tucked inside an unstructured dress or coat to impersonate a pregnant woman. To enlarge the face, insert grapes (or other soft fruit) into the top cheeks or jowls.

For a leaner appearance, simply adding a few inches of height (using the techniques above) can create the illusion of a slimmer frame. To thin the face, consult "The Art of Disguise: Makeup" in Casebook No. 2.

And don't forget the detective's most convincing technique: self-assurance. If you don't believe in yourself, surely others will not believe in you. Be clever, be thoughtful, and be convincing!

— ACKNOWLEDGMENTS —

Our deepest thanks to our agent and dear friend, Gail Hochman; our wonderful editor, Lisa Sandell; her assistant, Jody Corbett; art director, Steve Scott; fact-checker, Dr. Nancy Workman, Chair of the Lewis University English Department; and Ellie Berger, for her support in countless ways.

Thanks also to our friends and family for putting up with our disappearances, and to Ruby and Levi, the magic in our every day.

ABOUT THE AUTHORS

TRACY MACK is the author of two celebrated novels: *Birdland*, a Book Sense Top Ten Book, a Sydney Taylor Award Honor Book, and an ALA Best Book for Young Adults, and *Drawing Lessons*, a *Booklist* Top Ten First Novel and a *Teen People* NEXT Award Finalist.

MICHAEL CITRIN is an attorney and has been a Sherlock Holmes fan since he was a young boy.

Together, Tracy Mack and Michael Citrin are the authors of the first two casebooks in the Sherlock Holmes & the Baker Street Irregulars series, *The Fall of the Amazing Zalindas* and *The Mystery of the Conjured Man*, which have been published in 26 countries. They are married and live in the Berkshire Hills of western Massachusetts, with their two children.